St. Louis Community College

at Meramec

Presented By

THE
CARETAKERS

Bernard Mathias

TRANSLATED BY
FREEMAN G. HENRY

VIKING

VIKING

Published by the Penguin Group
Penguin Books Canada Ltd, 2801 John Street, Markham, Ontario,
Canada L3R 1B4
Penguin Books, 27 Wrights Lane, London W8 5TZ, England
Viking Penguin Inc., 40 West 23rd Street, New York, New York 10010,
USA
Penguin Books Australia Ltd, Ringwood, Victoria, Australia
Penguin Books (NZ) Ltd, 182-190 Wairau Road, Auckland 10, New
Zealand
Penguin Books Ltd, Registered Offices: Harmondsworth, Middlesex,
England

First published in France as *Les Concierges de Dieu* by Bernard Grasset,
1982
First published in Canada by Penguin Books Canada Limited, 1988

Printed and bound in Canada

Canadian Cataloguing in Publication Data
Mathias, Bernard.
   The caretakers
Translation of: Les concierges de Dieu.
ISBN 0-670-82127-6
I. Title.
PQ2673.A74C6513 1988   843'.54   C87-094837-7

American Library of Congress Cataloguing in Publication Data
The caretakers   87-51630

To the Capricorns in my life
Geneviève
my father
and to my mother

The
Caretakers

The bees buzzed in the burning air. It sounded to me as if they were sizzling and their music was the music of all nature frying, trapped by the sun's white flames. The morning sun was orange and warm, and as it rose to a blinding height, it erupted and sent sparks hurtling earthward. Then all creation was afire, the meadow where I played was redolent, insects and flowers cooked together in the great cosmic oven.

Hidden in the tall grass, spared by the daisies still wet with dew, each day I witnessed the wanton burning. The sun favoured me, warmed me, awoke life in me day after day.

I was often alone in the vast meadow. Perhaps my mother or my sister were nearby, watching over me. But I do not remember anyone. I recall only the tall grass, the beetles and the lizards, the yellow wasps and the russet bees, the white orb that danced above my head and formed purple butterflies beneath my eyelids when I closed my eyes.

And each time the meadow was born anew from its ashes, I remained unmoving, transfixed by the sensual and consuming desire to grow, to fill out a little more each day, just enough to run farther, farther in the direction of the tall gate of the vegetable garden ringed by monstrous hornets, just enough to escape my daisy nest, to be recognized as worthy of life by the entire world.

His eyes shining with obstinate pride, he had placed before me a thick, dark book. I leaned forward in my chair to examine the time-worn leather and the gilt-edged pages. Soon I would have to take up this book so heavy that only my father could manage it, to recite it from end to end without an error. I sensed, beneath the miracles it solemnized, movements and cries and above all, in the last pages, chaotic flights and a terrifying clamour.

But perhaps the clamour was not only beneath the thick, brown cover. I seemed always to hear it, even when the ancient book was put away, even when I listened to the bees sizzle. The clamour was inside my skull, and try as I might to look ahead, it was always there, tugging at me.

I knew. My good fortune in living in this patch of meadow came after a universal catastrophe.

I was the last child, the one who did not see the forest burn. But I knew. It could be justifiably written on the cover of the Book that I, and those like me — if there were any left scattered about the earth — were the survivors of a universe brutally annihilated on the eve of my birth.

Almost a spontaneous generation. A final miracle that no one had expected.

I could not allow myself to commit the error of enjoying it selfishly, gluttonously, of growing freely in the place toward which a fresh wind carried me. It would be my task, until the forest was renewed, to bear witness to the catastrophe. The terrible event that had just been appended to the Book was my burden, and it already prevented me from rushing carefree to scale the oak trees that shaded the garden pond.

I had inherited three first names: Daniel and Moshe, those of my paternal grandfather. And that of my mother's father, Elie.

Which to choose? One could not run after a child, calling out three different names. My sister Edith had the idea, so as not to slight the memory of either of the two martyrs, of joining the first syllable of each name:

"Damoel, Damoel, come darling...The wind is getting cold. Look, the tall trees are shivering and turning blue!"

Edith has beautiful brown curls that caress her dimples and shake like sleigh bells at the slightest breeze. She sits on the grass, her checkered, full-length apron tied tightly around her small waist and moulding her breasts, which I imagine white tinged with blue, fuller and warmer than Mama's when I press my face against them.

"Come now, come, my love. Papa and Mama are waiting. We mustn't worry them. Dinner soon. Dark soon, all dark — everywhere..."

I don't understand everything she says. I never know whether Edith is talking or singing; her words take flight with the evening breeze, and then that beast which thumps next to my ears, that gentle beast — imprisoned in her left breast — prevents me from hearing properly. Edith squeezes me so tightly in her arms that I am almost as warm as I was earlier, when I was surrounded by fire and light:

"...all blue, all dark — everywhere. The dormouse is going to sleep. The wolf awakens..."

Edith sings and the poplars applaud, shaking their tiny paper leaves.

Suddenly a yellow light. Noise, lots of noise. Bobby barks. The radio coughs, and a strange, far-off voice wends its way toward us against the winds and the tides, speaks to us in Hebrew, the language of the Book. Mama scolds us gently:

"*Gyermekeim*, my children...But where have you been? Why worry Mama? It's so late! *Istenem*, my God! Children, what trouble!..."

Mama does not speak the same language as Edith. In Hungarian her voice sings and groans. Edith, the youngest daughter, is already speaking the language of this country. She is progressing wonderfully in school and is teaching the new tongue to all of us, though she still speaks it with a slight cooing. Sometimes Papa and Mama speak to each other in a language dominated by heavy double *r*'s and gentle *oo*'s and that they alone understand. It is Romanian, the language of adult secrets and tense moments. But the laughter and benevolent tears of

Yiddish unite the four of us in a language whose words fuse joy with malice, like shooting stars that fall into darkness and fear.

Edith, Mama, the vast plain and the mountain in the distance.

Edith, Mama, the dog Bobby...As for my father, I remember him only vaguely.

One evening, however, his great man's paw seized me by the shoulders and lifted me up into the high chair. His pointed fingers pressed into the nape of my neck, as they had the habit of doing when he removed the cat from his path. The light hurt my eyes. Mama had disappeared into the bedroom with Edith. He spooned the food into my mouth and began to speak in the voice of *Kol Yisrael*, the language that came all the way from Jerusalem. He wanted me to repeat what he said. I had to learn right away the *lashon hakodesh*, the holy language, as well as Mother's tongue, and the language of this country, too. I had to. He became angry because I had forgotten the word "book."

"*Book*, it is very important," commanded the gaping mouth.

I choked on my potatoes.

"Everything, EVERYTHING is in the Book...*Am Hasefer*...Repeat, Daniel-Moshe: *Am Hasefer*, the people of the Book, we are the people of the Book."

The man's face came much closer. I could not swallow anything. His eyes, two small blue-grey marbles enclosed in the scowl of his joined eyebrows:

"Daniel-Moshe! Repeat!"

Tears swelled. My throat was pinched shut by a membrane that refused both words and food. He kept on stuffing and ·stuffing. The lever that had been holding everything back suddenly broke.

"Rozsa, he won't say it, he still won't, you know very well!"

A hush fell over the house, just as it does over the meadow and the forest before the sky drowns the earth with water.

I swallowed and swallowed. I could not speak or cry, or shout. The hatch opened wider and wider.

"Obey! You must obey your father!"

Could not to him meant would not. I would not say "*Am Hasefer.*" Those were his words. Impossible to make them my allies, impossible to make them mine. Even if upon those two words depended my freedom, my race toward my mother's arms, toward my blue-sided bed. I could not, even if this scene had to go on and on, even if my mother began sobbing and pleading gently. Would not. Could not. I swallowed and swallowed. My heart stopped. My stomach churned, then heaved. I choked. One arm gripped the chair. The other swung wildly in the air. I choked. Panic. Panic. I should not...and then: too bad, too difficult...A chalky mash splattered on my father's face and he drew back, trembling with indignation.

So many things to see...How to do it? Can a person live long enough to examine intensely every thistle, every pistil, every dragonfly?

My eyes open wide, focus, bulge out. The sun scorches my pupils. No matter. I must see everything, even the white orb whose flames blind me.

I already know that life has meaning, that the world is big, so big, and that it beckons to be known.

My father is wasting my time. My father crams me into a tiny room, into a miniature world where the printed word alone beckons, where books alone are to be acknowledged, observed, deciphered. Outside, everything is flaming and new; outside, everything is bright, vast, complex. I must run outside as far as the pond, as far as the wood, as far as the garden gate, farther still, into the distance where cars and birds and clouds disappear. As far as the eye can see...I must learn how to read, how to write, how to retain it all.

I want especially to trace the lines of space and the things that fill it: the clouds, grotesque dwarfs or mythical beasts; the flowers and the flies; the giant metallic insect that buzzes down the road, the road that leads to the unknown, to the big city...Yes, to get it down on paper as soon as possible: to draw a hill, a cricket, to make them hard and fast, never to forget them, in case, in case we have to leave again, to go away. Drawing: precise writing that is demanding, disturbing, maniacal. I do not know how to read the Book well. I have not yet learned by heart the *alef-bet*, the Hebrew alphabet. But I already know how to "write" the caterpillar, the water snake, to "write" Edith's feverish eyes and, with quickly mastered strokes, her temples, her thin nose, the roundness of her cheeks, to "write" without restraint and by the hundreds the large S's of her hair, to "write" them today in regular waves and another day in matted wool or lamb's fleece. Edith, laughing quietly, sees with eyes saddened from having seen so much. The stubborn little boy, to whose eyes all is still new, scrawls, shades, rejects, records, then suddenly abandons his paper, runs away to think, only to return quickly, to recompose quickly and, ever so quickly, to remember.

The Pardos lived nearby. Their daughter Sylvana was Edith's closest and dearest friend. They often went together to the wood, to sit on the moss and to confide in vibrant voices secrets and heartaches. I trotted along behind them from one oak to the next, stopping to observe a procession of ants, to scratch in the earth, to pluck the petals from a flower. Then we wandered over to the tumbledown farmhouse, which was as flat as an unrisen pastry. In the half-light, at the end of a long table, was an unalterable, silent silhouette coiffed in a beret and flanked by a bottle of wine: Old Pardo, who scarcely budged at our intrusion and laughter. He rose only to contemplate the victims attracted to the sticky ribbon hanging from the low, blackened ceiling. In the kitchen, the smoke from the pots obscured somewhat the heavy woman in the grey apron attended to by Louisa, who was only a few months older than I, yet already so solid, so vigorous.

She and I would set off toward the meadows. She urged me on as far as the muddy stream in which we splashed and played. Everything with the Pardos was calm, easy, delicious foolishness. In the morning, as I played on our front steps, I would see the old man in the beret go by. He would disappear into the forest and come back one or two hours later loaded down with boughs and branches and mushrooms. One day I followed him a little way and dared to ask him what he was going to do there. The man turned around, his brown, wrinkled face lit up. He waved a large fig leaf, squatted slightly and pretended to wipe himself.

"Those Italians are doubtless nice people," my father would say. "We shouldn't forget that they did us no harm during the war. But you mustn't lose sight of the fact, Edith, that they are pagans just the same, worshippers of idols. All the statues of Jesus and his myriad saints are nothing else! And their children are just like them. You only have to see how they live: not a book in their house, no tradition, no hygiene. They're peasants who wash only for holidays, like the ones back home in Transylvania. All they know to do is get drunk and then go to their church to be forgiven. God protect us!"

Mama would blush, sigh and then laugh, each in turn, as she did when we got away with something with Papa. How fortunate, despite all our misery, to belong to the people of the Book.

I understood vaguely that it was all right to despise these people; but it was too hard for me. I found Sylvana very beautiful: her milk-white skin, her blue eyes, her copper tresses. And Louisa: so smart, never short of ideas. I also liked the half-light of the room with the low ceiling, the flypaper, the odour of camembert, of wine and of forbidden smoked ham. And there was something else that I had been forbidden to look at, something from which I must turn away: a thin young man with long hair, nearly nude, crying, attached to a small boxwood cross above Louisa's bed...

In the evening, in my high chair, I soared above the three itinerant heads bent over their table. The old radio set sputtered voices and songs that were incessantly garbled by the reptile-like hissings of interference.

"They are doing everything to keep us from listening to our brothers in Israel. Ah! When will we cease to be surrounded by enemies! God has made us undergo terrible trials," Edith would intone in the voice she used when mystically inspired. "But you'll see, Mummy, you'll see, my little Papa. Now, now they'll all recognize that we are Goodness!"

My father's quick glance at her sufficed to say that she had spoken justly. There was a quick glance at me, too, to see whether the smallest fragment had succeeded in penetrating my strange mind. He got up to adjust the ailing radio and turned the knob. The needle on the illuminated dial traversed London, Budapest, Zagreb, Gibraltar, Algiers, stopping somewhere in a half-millimetre's space between Ankara and Cairo: "*Kol Yisrael*, you are listening to the Voice of Israel."

Here, in a dining room tucked away in an obscure French province, a tenth of a millimetre and contact is lost. The country promised to me is a minute measure no larger than a tenth of a millimetre. How small compared with the pond, the meadows, the mountain peaks that recede into infinity. And they, the three others who tra versed half a continent before bringing me into the world here, they dream of an asylum invisible and scarcely audible in the earth's immense symphony. And I, on my perch, I wait for my legs to grow so I can run in all directions, so I can hear all the voices of all the corners of the universe — without choice, without preference.

My father keeps vigil over my dreams. He also keeps vigil over my mother's silence. I sense that she is prone to caution, that she finds nothing inspired to add to her daughter's ecstasy, that her vital forces have waned, exhausted by hope. The man's glance passes from her to me. The Jewish mother, the one responsible for the children's upbringing, is supposed to be able to detect every little flaw, and yet she is infusing melancholy into the veins of the silent little newcomer.

And when she is guilty of letting me muse and draw, guilty of laxity, she clears the table quickly and disappears into the kitchen. Within the family nucleus, the orthodox are reduced to two: the father and the daughter, forever glued to the radio.

A last glance falls upon me, the cold glance of an expert inspector, the glance of a grown man who has become distrustful.

At that time the cinder road brought us other survivors, cousins or friends, not seen since the terrible reunions following the nightmare. They went out of their way to visit us before catching the boat in Marseille.

I had my first view of a blue-black tattoo on a forearm, like the ones on the meat that came to us from the kosher market in the big city. The din grew louder and louder as the radio coughed, the wind howled against the windows and the exclamations of horror or hope swelled, according to whether they evoked the recent past or the near future. I was carried into bed, tired and cranky. The others were afraid I might overhear accounts too terrible for one so young. But through the wall I heard all too well the frightening tales the men recounted in roaring voices while someone snivelled loudly.

In the morning, the pain remained purged for a few hours. The men went off to town. The women stayed and tried to affect the light-heartedness they had once known. They showed off their clothes and sometimes exchanged them. They laughed at having grown fatter and made their full bosoms protrude from their *décolletages* as a sign of refound health.

"Magda, come now. Please. Remember the child!"

"Don't worry. He's too young to understand."

"You know, Magda, he's as curious as anything."

"Already? So much the better, my dear!"

And warm, butter-soft fullnesses hugged me on the old sofa. If only that number had not been there, on the forearm...

"My little darling, my little fawn, my little love. How marvellous, a child so young. Rozsa, you're so lucky. Who would have dreamed a few years ago that there would be a newborn child among us? You were the first of all of us to become pregnant. Do you remember how we used to feel your tummy when you told us about it? Soon I, too, will have a little one of my own. Just enough time to get settled...All I ask is that there be peace between us and the Arabs. I don't want our children to have to fight. Ever."

My mother dabbed away a tear from the bluish semi-circles under her eyes:

"This little peepot, this fledgling, this little-bit-o'-nothing, carrying a rifle, *Got zol uphitn!* God protect me!"

She grew tense now because the other women were talking about the great event, the imminent departure, which was only a few days away. And all the while, my father kept repeating, "Before the year is out, when my work here is finished..."

Another three thousand kilometres beyond the sea: the oven of the Orient, bullets whistling in the streets, death awaiting those who dare to seek a crust of bread. All that before the year is out. When he was gone she found the courage to summon her fears with passion and conviction.

"Now Rozsa, it's obvious that you didn't experience the camps. Those who have survived can't stand to remain a minute longer on this rotten continent."

She took me from them and carried me outside. She envied their steadfastness, their militant strength of character, which her husband too often cited to her as an example.

I found Bobby outside in the peace and warmth of late afternoon. I also found Louisa, whose full cheeks seemed forever stuffed with bread and jam.

"Come. We'll go see Star."

She led me off to the stable, and we dreamed a while there in the half-light, next to the gentle mare whose countenance was brightened by a beautiful white patch on her forehead, between her eyes, like the jewel of a Hindu princess. Then we ran down to the vegetable garden. We hid under the tomato plants which smelled of basil, we tickled each other, we caught each other by the breeches, we examined each other — deliciously. While Bobby yapped hysterically and bounded on ahead, our galloping crushed the tender meadow grass beneath our feet. But the shadows were growing longer, and distant voices began to call to us. Louisa, the little giant, set off in enormous strides to rejoin her family.

I returned to my mother and her anguish:

"I saw you playing by the pond. People drown there, you know. You were playing with hornets. Their sting can kill a little boy. Never go down to the stable again. One kick from an idiot horse and that's it, the end. And stop rolling around in the grass. You'll break a bone. You're too young. You have no sense of danger. You fool around without thinking while I wait here and worry myself half to death."

It was impossible to play when she was like that. Edith was in school. My father was usually at his lessons or in the fields. And alone as she was, all she could do was to waste away with worry. Soon there would be nothing left of her at all.

I decided to heed her warnings and to learn fear and danger. Louisa would have to play by herself. Little goys and shiksas are born rough and tumble. We are not. I knew that my play would be ruined by her concern, by the fear of her fear. I began to stay close to her. Edith was teaching me to read; my father was instructing me in *lernen* (studying and deciphering the sacred texts), and in *davenen* (prayer). I was learning to fear: God, man, and all the rest...

The circle grew larger around the child who liked to draw. People applauded once he began to sketch profiles on the house walls with bits of chalk. It was a large house, full of boisterous happy-go-lucky youths for whom my father was responsible: he was preparing them for the *aiyah*, the "ascent" to Israel. In the morning, in improvised classes, he taught them Hebrew in the empty rooms on the second floor. In the afternoon, he recovered a measure of his own youth, which had been interrupted by the war. He worked with his charges in the fields, cut wood, looked after the animals, organized soccer matches. Everything was done according to the rule-book, including the group photo in striped jerseys.

These tanned youths were not really like us. Their names sang a cheerful oriental refrain oblivious to our pogroms. Their healthy, natural appetites shone through their smiles. Beneath the Maghreb sun of northwestern

Africa, they had learned to anchor their young lives, to
moor themselves securely to the land. The boys' legs were
placidly muscular, like those of oxen; their bare chests
glistened with strain and caused flutterings in the large,
red- or white-draped bosoms of the beribboned girls.
Their youth was turbulent and wild; they were ready to
rebuild a paradise. The summer was full of their squabbles and their games, their violence and their lust.

Toward the end of autumn, the preparation complete,
the happy savages bade us farewell with waving handker-
chiefs. Soon, on the winding road, the truck-bed was no
more than a small, multicoloured square from which the
wind brought us snatches of Hebrew songs, Zionist
marches or hymns to the glory of the newborn State.
Their comrade, Yohanan, my father, watched them disappear and dreamed of their destiny. "Next year in
Jerusalem," he muttered, "next year it will be my turn":
next year the Agency will reward him for his service to
Zion. Next year will find all four of us beneath the regal
blue sky of the Promised Land. There he will belong,
there he will be somebody. The Agency has promised...
Soon. Perhaps tomorrow. Fifteen years the same
dream...Marseille is so close, where boats are loaded to
the hilt with muscles and legs that ask only to defend, to
serve, to build. And perhaps he himself will become a
great man, he who only a short while ago was recognized
as that wonderfully precocious young teacher in a *heder* in
Transylvania: he, who, despite the censure of the elders,
had been the first Jonasz to pronounce the Sacred
Language without the archaic accents of the *shtetl*, thus

breaking with age-old tradition; he who was the first to know the new *ivrit*, "modern" Hebrew, paradoxically older still than the other and perhaps very much like that used by Joshua and his armies to voice their joy after having strung together victory after victory on the soil of Canaan.

Time had broken down. High above, beyond the clouds, the great invisible clock had fallen out of kilter.

The apprentice pioneers had departed. My father spoke of his age; it was time to "ascend" to Israel — now or never. Mama sank into a deep gloom: "No. No. Not yet. Not until there is real peace."

Papa was out of work. He was now gone much of the time, seeking out contacts. Edith was also away most of the day, at school in the distant city. A hush fell over the entire class when she recited Victor Hugo's poetry. Mama had learned about him long ago in her small Hungarian school during the days of Franz Josef, and that intimacy with the great poet led her to dream now.

A half-light caressed us, cajoled us, Mama and me. Mama. Your now-grey head bent over your inexhaustible mending. A little sigh, followed immediately by a song from out of the past. A past veiled in gas and smoke, so soon spent, swallowed up. A song neither gay nor sad. You at fifteen, a little Jewish girl from Budapest in your flapper skirt, the Argentine tango you sang in Hungarian while you polished the benches with your papa, a sexton. You at twenty, thin, cold, humming a gypsy tune, full of light-hearted despair. Soon you will be a woman, soon you will be at his side beneath the nuptial canopy. Now, now you think about your naked scalp beneath a hair-piece made from the tresses of an unknown woman.

"What are you drawing, my little pigeon?"

"You, Mama."

"Me, my love?"

"Your hair, why is your hair grey? Mama, are you old?"

"Old? You find me old, my little one...I'm tired. I have been terribly afraid. I have walked long distances. I have cried so much...But I'm not old. My hair began to turn white when I was twenty-eight. But at least it had grown back in. At least it was mine! Afterwards, I wore only my own hair. I refused to have my head shaved."

"Mama, the Germans, why did they shave your head?"

"The Germans? What are you talking about? No, it was the others!"

Who, then? Who did that to you?"

"When one of our girls marries, she is not allowed to keep her hair."

"They are punished? Why are they punished?"

"I don't know, my little chick, that's the way it is. It's been that way for generations. But you mustn't compare that with the Germans. *Lehavdil.* Believe me, there's no comparison at all."

My pencil point traced the tangles in my mother's hair. I tried to keep the conversation going.

"Mama!"

"Yes?"

"Edith showed me a woman in the street. She didn't even speak to her. She told me, 'You see that woman. She's Mademoiselle Levasseur. After the Liberation, she was shaved bald in front of the town hall.' Who did that to Mademoiselle Levasseur?"

"That's something entirely different, my darling. No, it was members of the Resistance. God knows what atrocities she may have committed!"

Another sigh. She began to sing again, in French this time. Mama learned a new language by singing. There had been Hungarian and Yiddish, then Romanian, a necessity when Transylvania ceased to be Hungarian. Now it was French. Soon it would be Hebrew. For the moment, she tried to imitate Line Renaud singing "*Ma Cabane au Canada.*"

"In any event," she began again, "as soon as the war broke out, as soon as they made us wear a yellow arm band, I told him: 'I don't know whether we shall be able to escape them, but I am not anxious to make myself stand out by wearing that horrible wig!' He had no choice but to accept. But the day I took it off, I discovered that my hair had grown back grey."

She turned on the lamp and laughed at my portrait, in which she recognized the troubled arc of her eyebrows and the tangles in her hair. A moth fluttered around us. Edith's whisperings stole into the room from behind the front door: the interminable confidences she revealed to Sylvana, her "friend for life." Papa would not come home tonight. We would not be forced to listen to the radio; I could draw for hours. And what's more, what's more, I would eat ham.

"Your children are prone to rickets," the doctor had said. Alarmed, Mama had implored my father to allow this temporary bending of the *kashrut*.

"Oh, Janos, only until we can provide them with a regular diet of kosher meat!"

He had taken down one of the heavy, ancient books, had thumbed through, had checked and rechecked.

"All right, Rozsa. If their health is in peril, it is permissible. And since he has not attained the age of *bar mitzvah*..."

This evening, my father is not home. I lay the beautiful pearl-pink slice over my mashed potatoes and sing out at the top of my lungs, "I love ham and I love sausage — "

"Damocl! How wicked! That is quite enough! If he should hear you, if he were here...!"

Then I smother her with kisses because there is no danger. This is an evening without restraints. We can be gluttons. We can let ourselves go. In all directions. Free. Free to explore. Free to enjoy. Free. Like other people. Later, Edith will open a book, a brand-new one, her literary anthology, and will teach me to read the characters which seem to have been invented only yesterday. She will recite Verlaine, will act out a scene from *Athalie*. Before going to bed, I shall listen for the twentieth time to the story of Monsieur Seguin and his nanny goat's exhilarating escape to thc mountains, to the freedom and the grass she loved so well: "The grass was so much greener there." And, as usual, I shall fall asleep before the wolf eats her.

From time to time my father hoisted me onto his motorbike. He drove me to the wood where hazelnuts were gathered and promised that before long I would have a pocketknife all my own. He spoke little, his mind absorbed by that other place I had never seen. I waited for him to notice me, to touch me, to acknowledge my presence next to him. But he remained absorbed, distant, far away, as his knife hacked its way through the brush. Once in the clearing, I tried to make myself inconspicuous beside him. Finally, I chanced a few questions about the trees and the animals, the rain or the pond. I knew the answers. It was simply for the sake of a safe conversation. He did not answer. Perhaps he was not aware of his surroundings. Perhaps my questions bothered him. Perhaps, too, he rejected all that, just as I rejected the Book.

One morning the outing was shorter than usual:

"You are old enough now. There is no reason for you

not to go to school. You will be with little goys. All I ask is that you don't forget where you come from and that you don't forget which is your God."

Soon I was led into a vast courtyard amidst the impassioned shouts and blows exchanged by a multitude of little brutes whose language I barely knew. Inside, in the classroom, silence reigned. We scarcely dared look at the terrifying hippopotamus of an instructress. She had no face, only a grey-black mane and an immense, lipless mouth from which spewed suddenly a horrendous bellowing. The reaction was immediate: some fought back tears, others stammered or convulsed, a few squirmed in their soiled undergarments.

One day I was seized by a terrible nausea. I got up and ran toward the door. I heard her yell at the top of her lungs. But I was already out of reach, and soon I was cradled in the shelter of my mother's lap.

"Never again, Mama. Please don't make me go to school. Promise you won't! Promise!"

"I promise," she said.

"You're bringing him up to be a sissy!"

She had told him about my nausea and my hives, had shown him the welts. He conceded, grumbling. And I remained home, in the safety of our yard, to play with the cat and a chicken.

One day he came up to me, smiling:

"Shall we go, my son?"

"Where?"

"To the wood, as usual."

The sky was a greyish-blue, the colour of fine porcelain. A warm breeze played in my hair. It was morning, a little earlier than usual. All was quiet.

"Come. Let's go, let's go, now."

How rushed he was today. My mother's fingers buttoned my coat. Her hands trembled as she pulled down my beret.

"Hurry, my little one."

"Are we going far today? Are we going to another forest?"

"Don't ask questions. We're going, that's all."

The motorbike coughed, spat, leaped into the warm air of early autumn.

"Where are we going? Where are you taking me?"

The eyes and ears of the robot were closed. The robot knew where we were going, but refused to say anything. It seemed that the motorbike itself had changed today, had lost its animal grace, its ability to leap from bush to bush. A jackhammer clattering came from the motor as it forged stubbornly toward its destination.

I began to understand. I wanted to get off, but robots travel fast over the blacktop. I cried out, howled, struggled. But everything I grabbed onto, everything into which I sank my nails, turned into a steel centaur, a bewitched golem on autopilot. Rage and terror. Never again will I believe you. The mechanical man smiled. His steel appendages lifted me down. Mission accomplished.

The mechanical man smiled at the hippopotamus waiting at the gate.

That day I repeated aloud, "I do not love my father, I do not love my father, I do not love my father."

I have thus committed the supreme transgression: If you do not love your father, you do not love God, of whom he is the image on earth. It is the fifth commandment: "Honour your father and your mother, all the days of your life." I shall therefore die young. I have no right to life.

Now I understood. I understood why he looked at me suspiciously, and his silence when I asked questions. He knew, perhaps all along: the imposture, the monster in me. In order to survive, I would have to pretend to go along with things. Now, more than ever, I wanted to know the world. Now, more than ever, having torn aside the veil so soon, too soon. Provided I can stay long enough. Provided I am in a position to leave before I am ejected. Already a great distance separated my mother from me. Never could she imagine that such a horror could germinate in the mind of her son. And Edith! Father was her hero. She would never tolerate this heresy.

And so they moved slowly away from me. I would have to go it alone, to return at regular intervals to deceive the family with the type of falsehood one encounters in studying the *Tanakh*, the Scripture...Sincere in appearance, deceptive in intent, before leaving for good.

They have said: He is a dreamer, he enjoys his own

company, he will be an artist. God grant that he not turn out like his uncle, that he will recognize the serious side of life.

One morning he returned home downcast. His head in his hands, he spoke of work, of subsistence, of responsibility. Then his eyes came to rest on us, the noncontributors, the good-for-nothings, the *shlemiel.*

And the other two, leaning over him, caressed furtively, warily, his large, bent back. They said, "It's all right". They said, "Have strength." They said, "Thank you." He sat up slightly.

"The ingrates...after all I've done for them. In Romania I helped many of them, Jews, get over the border. I saved many from being deported to the camps. And later I educated and trained them, the new pioneers... Now I'm too old, or so it seems! Or else I'd have to accept anything at all: picking oranges, working in a factory. A failure. Like your brother!"

Mama sobbed, ashamed of her sole surviving brother, a poor, debt-ridden no-good living in some unseemly suburb in Tel Aviv. She ran to the kitchen once again, to hide.

"You," he cried out from his place at the table, "just as soon as you know we're not going...If you had let us leave with the others in '46, if you hadn't been so spineless!"

She confronted him suddenly, looked him squarely in the eye with a rush of assurance. She said, "I was exhausted." She said, "I was pregnant." She said, "Peace had come again, there was chocolate, there was fruit, there were friendly faces." She said, "So many of my loved ones were exterminated, I did not want to expose my children to another war."

His angry breathing betrayed his silence. The father and the daughter scowled, embittered, reproachful. I clung to my mother. The son, who each day reminded him more and more of that useless uncle.

She and I who desire secretly to put down roots. They are so much stronger than we, Mama. But who knows? Perhaps we shall win in the end.

He said, "In any case, there is nothing left for us to do here. We might as well go to Paris. At least there I know some people who can help us."

Mama dared not show her joy. Another delay. Palestine (as she insisted stubbornly on calling it) could wait a while longer. Paris. The City of Light. Even Edith's eyes sparkled with delight. Immediately the three nomads busied themselves with the determination of the date of their migration. How familiar they were with the process!

A few quick glances around the room, and Mama had already mentally organized the move.

"First of all," he continued, "what will we be leaving behind? An old house that's falling into ruin. There is nothing to keep us here!"

Edith blessed our departure with a quotation from the Book of Ruth: "Wherever you go, I will go; wherever you lodge, I will lodge; your people shall be my people, and your God my God."

But where are we going? Won't one of you three excited people please tell me while you pile sweaters and blankets into mounds? Mama, surely you will tell me, since you are less deluded than the others.

Yes, but where is it? I heard what you said. It is not the Promised Land. I was prepared for the scent of orange groves, for the sacred mounts, for rivers flowing with milk and honey.

"Not far," did you say?

Not far. Oh, in that case we shall come back. Come back to roll in the grass. Come back to crush chamomile pods. You say nothing more. And the others do not even hear me. I begin to believe that we shall not come back at all. Last night someone said, "The little one doesn't know what it means to leave."

To leave is to never come back. You see, you see. At least I know that.

We are now leaving the house where I was born. They do not even stop to look at it one last time. Only a quick pause to kiss the *mezuzah* as they go out the door.

He struggles with the heavy, yellow cardboard valises. Mama and Edith are again dressed in their migration clothes: frock-coats dating from the exodus, heavy ankle socks truncating their calves, hobnailed walking shoes — the ones they wore to cross Europe such a short time ago. It was only yesterday, Mama says.

For the love of God, tell me where we are going!

Not even a backward glance at the walls onto which the lamp had projected my shadow in my high chair night after night. Not a parting gesture to the tall oak tree I had renounced climbing long before. Not a sigh for the pond where I had tried to become a fish and from whose waters I had been pulled half-drowned.

He lifted me off the ground so that I, too, could kiss the *mezuzah*. But I was not allowed to taste the first cherries of May, nor to pet one last time my chickens, my rabbits, my cows. Those obedient and sedentary animals which, I now understood, had never belonged to me, which had belonged and still belonged to Louisa and her family.

I had believed until that day that I would grow at the same pace as the wild rosebushes next to the front steps, at the same pace as the tadpoles in the pond. In my drawings, whatever the subject might be, I had always found a place for everything that covered the earth, that filled the water and the wood. All of those things fitted invariably into the background.

"In a picture," Edith always said, "the most difficult part to situate is the background."

Not for me. Until now I had always found an animal, a hill, the tree trunk where we met, the tile roof of the farmhouse. I was there in my pictures, a miniature character, protected by a mosaic of familiar objects. I was no more than a pebble encrusted there, alongside many others.

It is time to go. Everyone is frantic. Put a string around this. Strap that down. Now we must uproot ourselves, pull ourselves from the earth, intact. Pull hard, hard, as one would pull a young and vigorous shoot that does not come readily. Something was going to change in me. I was learning to turn my eyes away from everything that had been my intimate world, everything stable and faithful: objects, creatures, people...

Soon, like the three others, soon, I would no longer have what they call *zitsfleysh*: the trees, the clouds and the cities would soon disappear so rapidly behind me that it would be impossible to remember them.

Soon I would be the principal character in a picture entitled *Onward with the Wind*. And from this time on, I too, like Edith, would find it difficult to situate the background.

$\mathbf{P}$aris paralyzed me with fear and an inexpressible sense of disappointment: nothing but black stones piled upon black stones, walls stretching to vertiginous heights and then disappearing from view without the least suggestion of an escape route leading to a valley or a wood.

Our shadows, crushed and crumpled by the mute façades, skimmed over a long succession of grey, unvarying streets.

Trapped like a rat. I shall never get out of this maze. I turned toward her, the liar, the idiot who had led me to imagine monuments of pink marble and parks as vast as oceans. But, for the moment, she was busy trotting along behind the man who dragged the heavy valises and stumbled over empty bottles, sending them rolling noisily down the sidewalk. At last he decided to hail a cab.

Eight o'clock in the morning. My father examined the numbers, then stopped before a scaly door.

"Here it is," he ventured with a forced smile.

Until that day, he had always eluded questions concerning our future living conditions in the secretary's quarters on the top floor of the synagogue. Mama, confident and tired, followed him without uttering a word. I looked up at Edith. She tried to smile, but only succeeded in pursing her lips. Once inside the entrance hall, she took my hand and squeezed it tightly. We immediately ran into three or four elderly Jews in black hats and overcoats who were on their way out after *shachrit*, morning prayers. One old man stood out from the others, owing to his rosy cheeks, his pointed beard, and his beige suit. He walked toward us, friendly yet preoccupied. The others, in sombre garb, who were talking excitedly in Yiddish when we came in, had now become silent wax figures in the dark entryway.

"Rabbi Weiss, you doubtless remember our last interview, right here...*Ikh bin der Secretar. Sholem aleykhem.*"

"*Aleykhem sholem,*" replied in chorus the rosy-cheeked old man and the wax figures.

Then we were led up the creaky, narrow wooden steps of a decaying stairwell by the *shamash*, the sexton, who puffed noisily into his thick, brown beard.

"Jancsi..."

"Yes, Rozsa, what is it?"

"Is this it?...Is this where we're going to live?"

"Certainly. I never said it would be the Ritz."

Edith and I, still hand in hand, look into the tiny room, so tiny that for the first time I feel that my body occupies a large space. Past the threshold lies a single room, our only room, where we shall have to eat, sleep, study, and...grow. How shall I be able to grow here? With two steps of a frightened mouse, Mama is in the kitchen, a narrow strip of space with a sandstone sink in a corner and a French window looking directly onto the grey slate roofs.

"But where is...where is the toilet, the bathroom?"

"Bath? Bathroom? Come now...The toilet is on the other side of the stairway, a few steps above the landing."

No one budges. The urge is gone.

"But these must be temporary quarters. Tell me it isn't true. I can't bring up my children in this placc!"

"Listen. I am the secretary of an entire community now. I may be needed at any moment, day or night. My job requires that I or you or the children remain here to receive people, to answer the telephone. And you will have to fill in if I have to go away."

"Receive, you say. How can I receive anyone here without dying of shame? Oh, Jancsi, you remember our apartment in Kolosvár. It wasn't very large, but it was decent, well laid out, with a little yard. If I had known that in Paris..."

"Exactly. In Paris there is a terrible housing shortage at present. You should thank heaven that you have a roof over your head. And stop bringing up the past.

Besides, don't forget! It was your decision. All you had to do was to say the word and we would have gone to Israel. Now, now that I've finally found a *parnosseh* here, a position, now is not the time to complain."

He had spoken. We laid out as best we could the three mattresses awaiting us in a corner, then the U.S. Army blankets.

My mother unfolded them in silence. The trip had made her thinner, and like that, her head bent over her task, I noticed for the first time that her nose was a little too narrow.

"You'll see. You'll see," he exclaimed with feigned enthusiasm. "With a little furniture it will look entirely different. And look at this. I haven't shown you. Marvel of marvels, a window looking STRAIGHT DOWN on the sanctuary!"

And, indeed, through the strange dormer window, we could see into the depths of the old temple.

"Yes. And if the little one leaned a bit too hard on it, the way he scampers around, he could, *khas vekholile*, God forbid, fall fifteen metres and break every bone in his body!"

"Oh, yes, leave it to you...But you're forgetting one thing. You're forgetting that in this place only good things await us. A sacred place, night and day below us, a glance away. God has granted us this privilege. We live in the House of God. We are his guardians!"

"His caretakers, you mean..."

It was Edith who had blurted it out. I had been expecting her to take up my father's mystical expression of good fortune, but not that way, not that way at all.

Little by little the old synagogues of Paris began to function again. After the terror, the mass departures, the spectre of death, the survivors ventured back to the *beit midrash*, their place of worship prior to the chaos, and followed the paths leading back to their old *shul*.

Week after week, month after month, miracle after miracle came to pass: a wedding on the rue Pavée; a *brit milah*, a circumcision, on the rue Trévise; a *bar mitzvah* on the rue des Tourelles. Even a burial, a real Jewish burial, a wonder to behold. Children had grown older. A Talmud Torah, a religious instruction class, was to be formed; and here and there teachers and rabbis and sextons were being hired.

My father would be the teacher, the accountant and the caretaker of an aged vessel in need of being raised from the silt into which it had sunk. Over the long years, the entire building had become engulfed in the sediment in which it and its faithful had been forced to take cover. The wood of the benches was discoloured, a wretched beige velvet curtain covered the Holy Ark, the cabinet that used to contain the scroll of the Torah. In this austere disorder, nary a graceful line, nary a motif, nary an inscription. First things first: convene a fund-raising committee, then repair, replace, beautify the benches. Soon a scribe appeared: young, long-bearded, in a black satin caftan and wide-brimmed hat, a stranger. He sat down at the table and began to draw, feverishly yet without an error, the beautiful black block letters — the velvet of India ink on ivory parchment. No one heard him speak. A strange force emanated from him, imposed a hallowed silence on the space surrounding him. He was far removed from those who watched, covered in the golden dust of the biblical past...Soon the Holy Ark welcomed these newborn texts swaddled in a scarlet velvet, somewhat too ornately embroidered in gold thread. The sombre curtain of wretched beige was replaced by a heavy and luxurious drape glittering with multicoloured spangles. We alone were party to the secret: it had been furnished by the director of a nude revue, an old friend from Sighet, where my father had lived. The two had studied together at the *yeshivah*.

A few feet away from the silent scribe resounded the voice of the Lithuanian painter, Tourjanski. He had been given the task of decorating the temple. In a strange Yiddish, difficult for the others to follow, he related stories and faces from his youth in Montparnasse: a malicious little genius called Chagall, a tall, sombrely handsome young man named Modigliani...Tourjanski was part artisan, part artist. With equal devotion and commitment, he could patch the cracks in the plaster or conceive the frescoes for the partitions of the women's balcony. Perched on his ladder, he created the religious fauna that so enchanted me, each animal the symbol of one of the twelve tribes of Israel. At night I dreamed that the temple was a silent, mist-enshrouded wilderness. I saw the lion of Judah spring from the painting and stalk in the depths of darkness the valiant stag of Naphtali.

Amidst the odour of fresh paint, the number of worshippers grew larger by the day. In the morning, following prayer service, they wound their way to the small room at the back, where they found a few simple wooden chairs and a long table set with dishes and unmatched glasses. It was a time of humble fraternity, the morning *kiddush*: slices of slightly stale *leykekh* — the long, pale sticks of *Shabbat* cake — followed by a familiar toast, *lehaim* (to our life). When the hubbub rose to a boisterous pitch, the rabbi tried to quell it, assisted by the sexton, who pounded on the table and issued a reproachful "sh, shhh, shush." They quieted down then, even the oldest and most talkative, like schoolboys caught making a disturbance. The rabbi would place on the table one of the enormous volumes that adorned the shelves, brought to us from the ancient *shtetl,* having traversed two or three centuries, four or five countries and numerous massacres along the way. The old man's reading was sometimes troubled by a fit of coughing. His beard would bob up and down until he regained his composure. Sometimes a word caused him difficulty and a moment's hesitation. Then came the ritual of questions, answers, commentaries, and commentaries on the commentaries. When the lesson was finished, they went back to their workshops, their jewellery shops, or their grocery stores, and, as they went, a few more words of Yiddish could be heard along a Paris street beneath the fading sky.

Under a white-gold sun, I emerged in the middle of the *Pletzl,* Paris's first Jewish quarter.

Friday morning. The Jews are busy preparing for the Shabbat: wretched people, like the dwellings that surround them. Here no one is decked out like the president, the *gaboim* or the other benefactors of our otherwise modest *shul.*. An old grocer in a cap offers herrings marinating in an old barrel and carps wriggling in a large basin placed on the sidewalk. Across the way, Monsieur Gutman, the record dealer, calls to Papa:

"Come, come, Monsieur Jonasz, I have a pure delight for you: this Moishe Koussevitzky, a prime recording...and this, too, a Sholem Katz, a thirty-three RPM!"

We come away with several bundles: prayers and incantations, the wailing of a people; and songs, too, lulls in the storm — light-hearted and malicious. Later we shall listen to them, later we shall sink into an irresistible and doleful pleasure.

He always ran into two or three friends from back there, from before, who seemed to me to be nearly a hundred years old. These old men in tattered, faded clothes, these poorly groomed women without makeup, looked just like the ones in the photos from the past, taken on the eve of the disaster. And scarcely was there a child to be seen in the neighbourhood.

It was there one evening, in the little, dimly lit room, that we celebrated the Paris visit of a venerated rabbi. My father placed me at a corner of the table, between two of the old men who were said to be of noble cast: men with broad shoulders, knotty limbs and the faces of Michelangelo sculptures. But I squirmed amid the heavy odour of schnapps, amid their Yiddish which passed so quickly from a murmur to a harsh roar as they rocked and recalled their days at the *yeshivah*, a movement so nervous and so rapid that their contours seemed to blur in the half-light of the smoke-filled air. Their words had to strain to pierce the atmosphere heavy with unintelligible words, stifled cries, desperate appeals from out of the past.

These rabbis frightened me, these bestowers and recipients of miracles. And, somewhere within the folds of their dark coats, I felt sure, death lay in wait.

Right next to me, close, too close: their watery eyes creased by the smoke, their olive skins. All these people in a hole-in-the-wall filled to bursting.

I was always frightened by Jews who resembled the ones in those accursed photos: long beards, black caftans, large hats — announcement photos or line-up photos. I did not want to see them assembled like that, penned up, even voluntarily. I wanted them to keep their distance in the vast world, to have room, so much room that they would not have to run the risk of meeting one another, so that no one would ever be able to recognize them again, to round them up...I knew they gathered together for mutual warmth, to hear the news of those who had survived, to relive. But I wanted no part of it; I could not see, sense or understand this need to begin again, to continue, this renaissance, this hope forever born anew that made me fear a new peril: the flames reached out to grab me, here, next to them, with them, once more...Soon the Nazis would be knocking on the door. The clamour would break suddenly into a dizzying silence: a perfect entrapment. And we would be forced to go back down the stairway, heavily escorted...

The year following our move to Paris, I contrived not to go to school: temper tantrums, hives, nausea. The abrupt confinement to the House of God was a shock for me. The idea of mingling with little goys, whose horizons were so vast and whose manners were reputedly so uncivilized, made me tremble. My ancestral fears were coming to the surface. Yet the thought of being enrolled in a Jewish elementary school, of being subjected to a reproduction on a children's scale of the life I led at home, made me panic even more. Children are such ruthless judges, such savage informants, such abominable spies. Besides, I had quite enough to do: all those services and prayers, all those faces, those constant intrusions into our lives, not to speak of the Thursday and Sunday morning *heder* in which I must strive, both in *Mishnah* and in Hebrew grammar, to be the very best.

Edith's studies had suddenly taken a turn for the worse. In Paris, in the eyes of the young French Jews of old family standing, she was nothing more than an odd and overblown *romanichelle*, a gypsy. She was quickly overwhelmed by it all. Fortunately, she had passed the age of compulsory schooling. Thus, without having to graduate, she was able to escape from that temple of forced culture and decorum...She would be a *tragédienne*, a poetess, a painter or a singer. For the time being, my parents did not flinch at Edith's glorious vision of her destiny. If it seemed difficult to imagine an illustrious artist among the ancestors of the *shtetl*, the very idea of a woman going to university was unthinkable.

Moreover, it would soon be time to marry her off. Was that not the most dignified of careers? "*A gite balabuste un a git yidishe mame, un nakhes fun di kinder*": A good housewife, a good Jewish mother and children who give you joy.

Sadly, such was not poor Rozsa's lot. With the passing months, she grew despondent from living in what had to be called a hovel with a sandstone sink and from the daily chore of heating large basins of water for washing and bathing. All that while the most *proste*, the crudest of the congregation's gossips, found it quite normal to have a spacious four-, five- or six-room apartment, complete with bath and central heating. Our quarters were so small, so uncomfortable, and we children became so nervous, so disorderly, so unstable. Each day the room was filled with outbursts spawned by our father, who would invariably say, "I have to go downstairs now; it's time for services."

He was the king of a small nation. That is how he saw himself when, in the dusty office, he granted an audience to the devout and the fervent, to the humble, to the rich, to the beggars who came to pour out their travails, large and small: an incessant procession of the homeless, of illegal aliens, of the embittered and the lonely, who often languished there until the call to *minha* at the end of the afternoon.

In fact, he had become what some had had in mind for him, the do-it-all of the synagogue: maintenance, book-keeping, enrolling children in the Talmud Torah and the Hebrew class, preparations for the *bar mitzvahs,* treasurer, reserver of seats for high holidays, food co-ordinator for the *kiddush,* secretary in charge of distributing typed minutes of each committee meeting, decoration of the synagogue for weddings, sick calls and even preparing the dead...

When he allowed himself a few moments to chat with an unoccupied member of the congregation in the room at the back, he plugged the office telephone into our line, in the apartment. Inevitably, it rang: requests for information, urgent messages or, from time to time, outbursts and threats from some "Jew hater." Then our voices caterwauled throughout the building, as one of us rushed down the stairway in a frenzy in search of him. We were always there for anyone and everyone. As agreed, each of us shared this limitless profession.

They were already so distant, the days of soccer matches and excursions by motorbike, that short period of time during which we had been able to forget that being

Jewish meant perpetual self-discipline. The secretary was growing older by leaps and bounds. He had dredged up out of his memory the gestures and formulas of times gone by. He had abandoned modern Hebrew for Yiddish, since in Paris Hebrew was the sacred language, fixed forever in the sacred texts...Israel had finally disappeared from his dreams. He was becoming like all the others, a fervent Zionist, certainly, but one who, by some mysterious calling from out of the depths of time and tragedy, was destined to remain riveted to Europe. Israel lost each succeeding day a measure of reality. Israel was again becoming the indispensable myth. Like all the others, after the *seder*, the evening Passover service, he repeated, "Next year in Jerusalem." But something in him now prevented him from leaving. This quarter that was being repopulated with Jews so much like those of his youth? The specific role that he felt called to fulfil here: the resurrection of a community that so recently had been condemned to death? These Ashkenazi rites that had been nurtured by perpetual exile? The Yiddish that must be saved, that would soon be lost, forgotten in Israel?

Israel, the Hebrew State. Like his new friends, he cajoled from a distance, "Next year in Jerusalem." Like the old men from here, he would go there one day, to die there. To die in the Holy Land, that was the sole *aliyah* he now dared to imagine.

Why did he pretend to still believe in it? In preparation for the Great Departure, he sometimes bought household appliances, because "they are in short supply over there." Hence, the strange piston-action washing machine, already outmoded, that we were formally prohibited to touch until the Departure. The little space we had was thus further cluttered by all the objects whose only purpose was to remind us that, for others, Israel still had a concrete existence.

So, along with him, we began to dress our parts. It was not hard for Mama, who, relieved finally to have a place to unpack, agreed to lengthen the hems of her skirts and to wear a hat when she appeared at services. Such minor inconveniences were not responsible for the growth of her permanent shame and frustration.

"This apartment...This apartment...I want to die every time someone comes to call...At my age...I never would have believed...In PARIS...An honourable position. Fine. But without the slightest semblance of dignity..."

He would say, "Don't complain, *abi gezint*, as long as we have our health...You'll just have to make do. To stay on the premises is our job, it is our plight to share, the four of us. And if you don't help me, they'll get rid of me. There would be plenty of candidates, you know."

I am still a kid, a child. I am not even close to my *bar mitzvah*. That leaves at least a little time...

But since I have been in Paris, an ashen cloud has hovered over me. Mama takes me in her arms to comfort me.

"We have lost so many children. Do you understand? They killed them. Almost all of them. My brothers' and sisters' children, every one. Twelve, fifteen, twenty, I don't know. Children like you and your sister. You are the last, you understand, the last children in the family."

She puts down her embroidery and restrains the unruly child between her knees.

"Later, Damoel, later, you must remember all this. You must never forget. Promise me you'll never forget."

I try to feel Jewish. Truly Jewish. I mean, responsible — inheritor of all the dead. I am learning little by little. It is not easy. At night, in order to fall asleep, I issue a call for help, to my mountains, my chickens, Bobby, Star, and also Louisa and Old Pardo...But the peaks are growing hazy in my memory. Star has begun to look like an ordinary horse in an ordinary western. And Louisa is gone, disappeared. Why should this terrible thing happen to me all of a sudden? Is it destiny? Why must my life stop here and now, my freedom, my fun?

Ghetto-Paris imprisons me, locks me up tight. Paris, where they have gone backward, all of them — Papa, Mama, Edith — returned in time and space to the east, to Sighet...They are at home there: the same odours, the same songs, the same Yiddish nostalgia, and, hidden away in the heart of the great city, the same *shtetl*, reconstituted. I, the only one born here, it is I who have been displaced, uprooted. And now I must learn those strange odours, those voices that frighten me, those new customs.

I try. I try to feel Jewish. I try to be like those who have suffered so much. Is it not the least I can do, to suffer with them?

Without realizing it, I experience daily a hundred little traumas. Am I going to be late to morning services? Will Sunday's lesson at the *heder* be very difficult? When I set the table, did I mix up the dishes for meat and those for dairy products? Have I left a drawing lying about — a woman's face, a bird, a silhouette — which might betray my frivolousness? Will he be upset today because I did not answer properly some congregation member's thorny question on the Bible? Will I make him ashamed because I am still too much like the Damoel who loved the pond and the elm trees?

Soon they will have me completely in their grasp. Soon I shall be properly moulded, as he likes to say, at the Jewish school.

In the meantime, I wear on the crown of my head and for the length of the day that obstinate skullcap that is forever falling off. My right hand writes or draws. My left hand serves only one function: to shove aside a hundred times a day, automatically, the excess Judaism, *yidishkeyt*, which cannot force itself on me.

I had gained a few months before having to face again the unsavoury odour of inkwells and freshly sharpened pencils. But my reprieve came to an end and the beginning of the school year confirmed my fears: the impossibility of adapting to the atmosphere of the Jewish school, to the old scholars in black skullcaps.

"Do not make me ashamed," the father had said. "Above all, do not make me ashamed. There, as here, the community will have its eyes on you."

The long ride to Paris's leaden nineteenth arrondissement...Every morning with Mama...So early...So far...Too young to take the métro alone...During my eight-hour exile, I watched the other kids enjoying a real and wonderful childhood: squabbles, wild laughter, howls, fights, tattling, bullies and willing drudges...Their eyes sparkled with eagerness and pride when the subject of tradition came up. How happy they were to be like their parents, to be with them, to lead the same life as they, to make the same gestures as they and at the same moment, to have the same ceremonies, for a lifetime...It was the *Talmud Torah* on a large scale, a dress rehearsal for the *yeshivah*. And I could think only of the arrival of the grey curls outside the iron gate at half past four: Me, a funny little classmate...who remained tight-lipped during religious instruction, but who recited by heart Lamartine's *Méditations* and sometimes ventured a question or two about the kings of France. A funny little Jew.

At last came the deliverance.

"What have you eaten today?"

"Nothing."

"Nothing at all? Not a little meat? *Edes Istenem*, good Lord, what will become of you?"

The two strays would get lost in the corridors of the métro, where, one day when they got off before the train had stopped, they fell flat on their faces...In such a hurry to get off, to get out...Too complicated...Too exhausting...

They begged and implored. The father gave in, finally, and allowed them to try a public elementary school in the quarter. Once again, he would have to blush before the members of the synagogue, and insist on his concern for the child's health.

At the public school, the stateless boy's interest in the

splendour of French heritage received approval...I went from services to class. The teachers were quite understanding on the whole, but I had to explain to them why I was not allowed to touch pen or pencil at Saturday class, nor even to carry my things home. Israelite or not, God must have been an Ubu-esque tyrant to have invented such absurdities. Better still, it was ample proof that he did not exist at all. How right they were to be the promoters of a France both enlightened and atheistic...

"Damoel? What the devil is this barbarous name? Couldn't you be called something a little more normal?"

"Daniel, Moshe, Elie."

"Daniel! Daniel, of course! At least it's a good French name. Very well. And then, what are you doing in class, in front of your teacher, with that beret on the back of your head? Haven't you been taught that isn't done?"

"Damoel! Damoel! *Sheym dikh!* Shame on you! What is this new foolishness of going about the house bareheaded? Little pagan! *Sheygets!*"

"It's Monsieur Dupanloup. In class, we aren't allowed to cover our heads. And, also, he said that you should call me Daniel. Because it's a French name."

"It is obvious that your poor Monsieur Dupanloup has never been to the *yeshivah*...Daniel. My judge is the Eternal God, in good, clear Hebrew...And Daniel, the Daniel in the lion's den, he was a *Franzos*, perhaps? The Old Testament, they revere it, too, you know. A teacher who doesn't even know his own religion! Ach! It's beyond me!"

Gilbert Lablénie sat next to me at school, Lablénie, a fountain of questions:

"Why do you always wear that beret when you're outside? In which language do you and your mother talk? Why don't you stay and have lunch in the canteen? And why don't you come to school on Saturdays any more? And when we line up outside to come in, why do you throw up every time?"

This last question was by far the most difficult one to answer: the teachers were nice enough; and my classmates, though rather brutal, had not yet stooped to anti-Semitic remarks. The vomiting was therefore a grave mystery repeated almost daily five minutes before going into class. Sometimes it was possible to hold it back, but not for long. And then it was catastrophe in the middle of class: sneering laughter, cleaning women, sawdust and towels. The worst trial remained that monstrous bottle of milk which some well-intentioned high government official (a Jew!) had the sadism to impose each day on all the school children in France, twenty-five centilitres at a time. I was happily relieved when at least the variant, chocolate milk, was not distributed. That meant certain nausea. And Dupanloup was always watching.

"You may have to chuck it up, *mon petit père*, but you're going to finish your milk! Mendès has prescribed it for the health of French children, and he knows what he is doing."

A few hints of panic surfaced from time to time in my dealings with classmates. They were goys, after all, and with a goy you can never be sure. What if one of them decided suddenly to stick you in the eye with a compass? God help you. It would be useless to try to ward him off. He would only become more brutal.

The years passed, and I was still next to Lablénie, who still asked regularly the same questions with no greater success. In the late afternoon, we stayed to do homework together. Gilbert invited me to his house two or three times, but since I did not dare reciprocate, I still had no idea what the home of an authentic average Parisian might be like.

"Don't mix too much with them. With your weakness of character, you would run the risk of being assimilated, God help us! But, on the other hand, don't forget to work hard, either. In this cruel world, we have to be the very best. Otherwise, it is impossible to do anything at all...In the army of those anti-Semitic Romanians, do you know who was his captain's favourite? Your little Yid of a father! And why? Why, huh? Because he knew several languages, and because he was orderly and disciplined. Not like the savages in the barracks. You must understand that, my son. Be a good Jew. But conduct yourself in such a way as not to offend them."

Eight. Nine. Ten years old.

Before the assembly of pupils in the school courtyard, there was another assembly. Before the teacher's call to class, another call from within another world. Before the lesson on the Commandments, other commands to observe.

Shnel! Shnel! Father pulls me from bed still soft and warm from sleep. Mama pushes me toward the kitchen where a basin of warm water awaits me. She begins to scrub, to scrub me with the rough cloth.

Shnel! Shnel!...I go downstairs to pray with my father: *shachrit*, sunrise service. Outside, night surrounds us, cold, dank, misty. My classmates are still sleeping. It will be another two hours before daybreak.

For this class, from the abundance of extra words to know, of lines to learn by heart and to recite, of texts always to have fresh in mind, there is no respite. No sleeping in, no Thursdays or Sundays off, and there would never be any of that. The Eternal God is an inflexible master who excuses no absence, who grants no days off. And although he had granted himself the Shabbat so that He might be idle, for me it was the worst of days, the most demanding, the most exhausting.

"Come, come, come. Let's get going now. Don't make me ashamed. The Rozman boy and the Bornsteins are already there, praying at their fathers' sides. They don't have to be pushed, not they! And yet they had to get up in the dark to come all the way over here. And you who have the great fortune to live here, on the premises, you drag in after them... *Oy vey!*"

During services, I kept waiting for the door to open and for some pal to appear other than Bertrand Rozman and Joseph Bornstein, two young centenarians already stooped like their fathers, and such impeccable apprentices in the trade of being Jewish...I would hope to see Claude, for instance, whose father became homesick from time to time for his native city of Lublin.

With Claude, I could talk instead of praying. I could even get a snort of laughter out of him when the sexton, beside himself, turned toward us, rolled his eyes and hissed: "Shh, shhh, shush!" Claude, that lucky devil, lived in an enormous apartment with a TV, and he spent weekends in Deauville, where his parents rented the most expensive rooms in the most luxurious hotels. They travelled on Saturdays and observed only the most important rites.

"But there are no rites that are more or less important than the others. All of them must be observed equally."

Claude lifted his head with pride and fired a sententious dart: "My father is religious, not a fanatic."

That shut me up, but good.

That was exactly what my father kept repeating. My father, who observed all the rites but would not allow his *payos*, his side-curls, to grow. That was exactly what Rabbi Weiss said; he wore two curls discreetly hidden behind his ears but did not wear a caftan. That was exactly what Rav Nussan said, the Gabbai who wore a caftan but would not go so far as to fast twice a week. That was exactly what Rav Moishe Frey would say, even though he wore a caftan, displayed two long, silvery ringlets, fasted Mondays and Thursdays and never shook a woman's hand...

"O.K., Daniel. I have to leave now. Mama is waiting with a great meal: oysters, leg of lamb and mocha cake. And afterwards, I'm going to the rink with Jean-Pierre."

I stayed there a moment, frankly embittered. Oysters and leg of lamb, that is what shocked me the most.

But Claude, as was his usual Saturday habit, had not come (no doubt skating somewhere in Deauville, or gulping down oysters with his friend Jean-Pierre, under the approving eyes of Papa Kolski,who was religious, but not — not by any means — a fanatic).

Eight. Nine. Ten years old. Learn, learn without respite. And read and memorize and recite. Run from French history to the *Tanakh*, from dictation questions to the *Mishnah*, from La Fontaine's fables to the 613 *mitzvot* (our good deeds, acts of kindness), from the geography of the Paris basin to the *Rashi* commentaries, from civics to the *Gemara*, from the multiplication tables to Hebrew grammar.

A slave. A slave forever going in infernal circles, like a squirrel running round his exercise wheel. A slave scarcely relieved by a few hours of furtive sleep, by short, undetectable absences, a few moments of infinitesimal sanctuary in the long days that ended as they began. At the same seat, prayers almost the same — *minha*, at the end of the afternoon, then *maariv*, in the evening — before I could go upstairs to draw my map of the rivers of France and, after Moses' exploit of parting the waters of the Red Sea, learn about Vercingetorix rallying his troops against the Romans.

Then, only then, could I prepare my satchel for the next morning so that it could start all over again.

Eight. Nine. Ten years old.

But that was not all of it: the history of France, grammar and mathematics, the *Tanakh*, the *Mishnah*, the *Gemara*.

I had to live, too, to find a way to live between the tightly spaced lines of what was forbidden, the cannots.

Cannot buy a chocolate ice cream on the way to school because I have just eaten beef. For there is milk in chocolate ice cream. And it is written: "You will not cook the lamb in the milk of its mother." And who knows? Perhaps the ice cream I want so much contains the milk in which the lamb had cooked — I mean the beef I have just eaten...Who knows? And if someone should see me...It is safer to abstain.

Before, in the country, when I was younger, those things had not mattered so much. Here in Paris there were too many witnesses, the risk was too great. And that skullcap I had to put on as soon as I took three steps...Three steps are so quickly taken. It is easier not to take it off at all.

Cannot. Cannot forget for a moment. Cannot stop thinking, concentrating. Sometimes I neglected to kiss the *mezuzah* because I was always running, running from one world to the other, always late, always adrift between two galaxies: two schedules, two calendars, two systems. As a result, everyone knew about me, everyone agreed. As a result, my grade reports from both worlds always read in indelible ink: "Needs to improve, needs to improve, needs to improve..."

Eight. Nine. Ten years old.

Paris had not kept its promises. Paris had taken Edith from me. Very early in the morning, she sped off to her drawing class on the other side of the great city and came back to us more and more exhausted. Paris had effaced Mama, worn her down to the point of nonexistence. In the shadow of the father's omnipotence, she had lost her substance, she had become incapable of making the smallest decision without saying, "Ask your father."

And he, always there, reigning from his derisive throne, came upstairs at the slightest pretext to lay down the law. Never an hour without him, without the distrustful glance falling on the suspect son, the only son.

Without warning, I had been drawn into the masculine world of adulthood and subjected to the judgement of a father, of all the fathers, a thousand strong.

Thursdays and Sundays, *Talmud Torah* days. *Talmud Torah* on the third floor and, downstairs in the rabbi's study hall, the childrens' *heder*, to which the most devout families sent their sons. There were only half a dozen of us there, unearthing the secrets of the venerable black books printed a century before in Warsaw or Odessa. The boys congregated around the table, austere and attentive. With their large black satin skullcaps propitiously in place, they appeared even paler than they were. And I with them, just back from public school, still unable to pronounce Hebrew that way, with baroque Yiddish accents.

My gaze travels from the archaic letters to the window. I listen to the sounds of typewriters sending their messages from the other side of the courtyard.

"Daniel, *Du herst nisht...*You're not listening. *Vos vet zayn fun dir*, Daniel? What's going to become of you?...*Oy vey!*"

One day, I looked at all of them with an icy stare, a stare from the days of the great dread. I saw them all. The old rabbi dressed in grey, his beard, his small, round silver-rimmed glasses. I recognized all of them. The children, the napes of their necks protruding from their prayer shawls, singing their irreproachable ghetto Yiddish in a half-light struggling against the darkness. A sepia photo, an inky brown. Paris, 1957...In this narrow, decrepit room, someone had taken refuge during the war, hidden out. Paris, 1957... And they were still here, and they had not budged. Or perhaps they were ghosts, the same ones who came to haunt me at night.

I got up. I tried to flee, but before I was able to make it through the doorway, my father grabbed me by the arm and pulled me back toward that *heder*, back toward the days of the Holocaust. I broke free. A mad, fearful chase amidst the lecterns in the sanctuary, the father breathing down my neck. I bounded from one bench to the next and leaped over the *shulhan*, the Torah table... All of a sudden, Monsieur Schneider appeared. Cornered! Two of them now to track down the renegade in the House of God.

The other held me securely. My father told him, "I leave him to you."

"I leave him to you," my father said on his way out, and the blows fell from the open hand of a stranger, whose fingers trembled with sadistic pleasure as he pinched me until he drew blood. I cried out because it hurt, but more so because my father had betrayed me, had conferred upon others the right to judge me, to punish me, while he hid behind the closed door of his office. Neutral and appeased. Matter resolved.

I knew also that Monsieur Schneider was an important figure in our little kingdom, and that he could be very helpful in time of need. By allowing him to punish me, my father had established an intimate bond that might one day serve him well.

Father, all the fathers, a thousand strong. In this quarter, security was tight. They ruled everyone, they would always have their say — and their way.

As a son and as a Jew, I was not...would not...could not, ever...be good enough.

In Paris, we had discovered the heavy solemnity of our holidays.

Sometimes their charm, as well: I liked the *seder*, the evening observances of Passover, which consoled me somewhat for not having Christmas, the trees and garlands not being part of our ritual. It was our *réveillon*, our holiday feast, but with the touch of sadness common to every Jewish celebration, every *simha*: bitter herbs, in remembrance of the years of slavery, took for us the place of *foie gras*.

Just the same, it was a joyous occasion. Mama put on her best dress, and Papa donned a long white tunic, the very one he had worn beneath the nuptial canopy. Since I was the youngest member of the household, my father addressed to me the answers to the four traditional questions of the evening observance. I also had the honour of seeking out the *afikomen*, a small piece of unleavened bread he had hidden somewhere in the room. Once I had found it, I had the right to claim a gift: a photo album, a jar of paint, a phonograph record. Around the table, the adults, full of nostalgia, recalled their childhood. This special event reunited friends and distant relatives, those we saw rarely, those who had avoided the drudgery of our rites but did not want to miss the childish delights of this springtime eve.

At *Simhat Torah*, celebrating the day God gave to his people the gift of the Law, the men danced: furriers, bankers, professors, doctors and simple artisans joined together in ancient fervour. They resurrected ecstatically a remote past, their eyes moist, their cheeks flushed from the carouselling of their turgid bodies, each one clinging to the other in an unwieldy *farandole.*

I liked *Sukkot* even more, the festival of "huts," for it was in huts that the children of Israel had dwelled while wandering in the Sinai. On the fifth floor, beneath the Paris sky and upon roof-tiles that we used in place of soil, we built a long *sukkah* with a ceiling made from varnished foliage. For a few days, a truce eased the tensions between my father and me. We busied ourselves calmly, adorning the leafy ceiling with beautiful pieces of fruit, Chinese lanterns and gold or silver cutouts that shimmered gaily above our heads. I painted panels in violent and babarous colours: plants and animals mentioned in the Bible, savage deserts, exotic skies. After services, the faithful ambled in, the most pious in their satin caftans, and sometimes a prestigious rabbi coiffed in his imposing mink-brimmed *shtraml.* They sat down and spread out on the table the food carefully prepared by their wives. Then came the prayer of thanksgiving.

"*Yo bo-bo-bom bim-bam bom-bom...*"

The Hassidic chants rose late into the night. Afterwards, we collapsed in a state of exhaustion; for to us alone belonged the tasks of clearing the table and cleaning up, to us alone befell the duty of readying the House of God for the morrow.

For others, the rites had retained their grandeur. They were the spiritual touchstones that made each day complete and added a glint of delicious mystery; they were a finely sculpted work of art, an aesthetic creation, a harmony of taboos and obligations; they were private conversations between man and his God — confidences magic and mystical.

I saw full well that this tender nonsense could be beautiful. I saw it in their eyes, in their dances, in their chants and in their moments of silence...

For them, for them, for them! But for us, the King of Kings' jesters, for us? Admit it, then! All that was nothing more than a run-of-the-mill job, a terrible grind. Admit it! What real joy did you find in it? I know, I know. People can't expect to be festive when they spend their lives preparing feasts for others. But why, then? Why try to make me love something you couldn't love fully yourself? No. That's wrong. You didn't want me to love it, you wanted me to learn it, to learn the trade, the servitude...You wanted me to become resigned to it, as you had, and your father, and your grandfather.

Listen to me. Being Jewish is not a trade, a profession.

Being Jewish doesn't mean a life of drudgery. Listen to me. It's a succession of rituals, you understand, a finely woven fabric of gestures, of caresses, an unrelenting murmur.

Listen. And what if it turns out that, of the two of us, I am the more religious?

That holy place was our gulag, and God was political obedience subserved by terror, the informant's terror: everyone spying on everyone else, everyone terrorized by the fear of being caught unawares. (And what if one of us decided to squeal?)

The other three had already gone mad, as would any dissident locked away under the pretext that an act of personal conscience is a crime against society — mad and feeble, as would any prisoner in a psychiatric ward whose rehabilitation therapy consisted of absurdities and lies...

I did not want to lose my own sanity. Not yet. I had to hold on, to wait and resist. It seemed like centuries before I would be in a position to flee, to get as far away as possible...And they had already made me believe that, should I be able to escape one day, even if I travelled thousands of kilometres and succeeded in convincing the members of a Masai tribe that I was one of theirs, there would always be someone there to denounce me, a KGB man disguised as a native, someone who would say that I had eaten crocodile or elephant meat.

I resisted with all my might...

But there were those moments of anguish when I felt

that, long before I could summon the strength to escape, their hovering madness would completely enshroud me...

Long and long and longer still,
After the poets have gone...

Charles Trenet sang with calm nonchalance. Sometimes it was Juliette Gréco, in a voice sweet and grave.

Place Saint-Germain-des-Prés. The girls were in black from head to foot. Black, their long hair cut straight across the front. Black, their narrow skirts slit up the side. Black, their open-toed pumps.

We went there, Edith and I, to be shocked by those strange fellows in plaid shirts whom our father insisted on calling "zazous," jazzniks, and by the girls who were treated as fallen women by all the wives in the congregation.

She and I went there to stroll amidst a new poetry — unknown, foreign, compelling. Then we returned home along winding streets, whose dim lamps scarcely lighted the façades blackened by time.

Then we reconstituted the pictures our minds had taken, memories of a trip to another planet. I rebuilt, stone by stone, the simple, dilapidated church while my sister followed again the graceful movements of the girls whose spiked heels beat a nimble rhythm against the paving stones.

She had enrolled in a fashion design course in the Palais-Royal section of the city, but that had to remain our secret. Each evening she brought home by the armful sketches of long-legged models, svelte and brassy. Her instructors encouraged her and called her a born artist. She began to believe it herself and to dress accordingly: tight pullover sweaters, heavy pendants, long hair cut straight across the front.

In a moment of excitement, she did a terrible thing: she took up playing the organ in a neighbouring church.

The parents no longer welcomed these talents, which smelled of sulphur. In the women's section, on holidays, Edith seemed quite out of place...Father began to fear for his job because of her silly notions. She must marry as soon as possible, he concluded.

Edith resigned herself rather quickly, told herself that she had been dreaming an impossible future. She dropped out of her classes, and we went no more to Saint-Germain.

Edith was growing up. Or, rather, Edith was growing older. Another cloud hovered over her, the fate of a girl in waiting. Her brief period of freedom had come to an end, gone were those two or three years beyond adolescence after which a Jewish girl must settle down — if nothing has happened — and take her place among the dried fruit, the leftovers. Twenty pairs of eyes during the week and a hundred on holidays examined her face for a sign, looked closely at the way she parted her lips, at the way she swayed her hips when she walked. Any suggestion of a glint in her eye or a pouting lip was as good as an announcement of a forthcoming *mazel tov*. Such indications gave rise to prognostication and rumour, and caused ears to bend. There was always a room full of people to cross. Whether returning to her room or going to the toilet, she had to make a path through them, to confront them, as they finished their *kiddush*. Twenty stares, a hundred seismographic readings recording incessantly, plotting out her life. She ended up adopting their obsession:

"When? When will I meet him? The one? Just to get the hell out, to get away from them. I'm going crazy, do you understand? At least with him I'll have a private life, something normal!

"Old maid! I'm an old maid!"

On her eighteenth birthday, in a fit of rage, she scored with her high heels the lower right-hand portion of the wardrobe mirror. The damage was permanent. Mama found a way to disguise it with a small, ridiculous gathered curtain.

Such outbursts became more and more frequent and frenzied. Afterwards, she hid behind a cloak of silence until the agony had subsided. Father consented to take her out from time to time, to *bar mitzvahs,* to weddings, to a chance concert given in support of a Jewish cause. He authorized lipstick, a new, more enticing hairdo and two or three new dresses.

But fair game was scarce: a few divorced men of tarnished reputation; widowers, grimacing and disconsolate old birds; an occasional adolescent stymied by his youth. Her generation was all but extinct — unless one searched elsewhere, far away in New York, perhaps, or in Israel. Nearly all the others, the survivors, had been shipped off to fight in Algeria.

On a *Shabbat* afternoon, in order to lighten the hours of required inactivity, we would both stroll over to a public square, like a miniature elderly couple, to sit on a garden bench and stare at the daisy-covered lawn. Before a blur of pansies, we rediscovered on occasion the delights of our distant past in the country.

I remember in particular one late afternoon we shared. A soft-spoken, lanky young fellow with glassy eyes talked to her about the desert, the Fallagha, the hostages, the unfortunate fellows on both sides of the war...A guy, not much older than she, who said, "What a bitch of a war!," who said, "What do life and death mean when you don't even have the right to decide?" Edith had been pleasant that day, strangely serene, sad and serene: because she was able to stay there as the evening shadows fell, because she was able to be herself without having to fix her hair or bat her eyes. Men, war, life, death, strong words, grave words, so grave that the refrain "get married, get married" did not seem so threatening.

They were to see each other twice. The first evening, he was in uniform. He approached her directly, with neither pleasantries nor the usual lines. He was calm and reassuring, like a big brother. He did not want to play games, his need was urgent. He was leaving that night and sought in her the last sweet resonances of a feminine voice, the silkiness of long hair, willing lips, the last he would kiss for a very long time, until the end, perhaps.

We met him again one September evening next to a Carpeaux statue. His eyes lit up for a brief moment. Yes, he recognized her; he was on leave for a few days. He began to talk and talk and talk. And, in the end, he concluded by saying, "In any case, it's beyond description."

I never breathed a word to the parents. She had not had to ask me. The young stranger remained a sweet secret between us. There was something nostalgic about it too: for a few hours we had forgotten the religious barriers. Neither he nor Edith had thought to mention it.

It was high time to respond to the invitations "improvised" by the *shadhanim*, the matchmakers, both male and female. It was not really a profession any longer, but rather a divine calling to organize get-togethers which might decide the direction of two lives, a means of perpetuating a tradition and, especially, of avoiding mixed marriages — a scourge, openly deplored, but nonetheless gaining ground. By dint of curtailing the unions of a Jewish girl and a Christian boy or of a naïve, misguided Jewish boy and a cunning shiksa who would not even want to convert, a marriage arranged according to custom had become a veritable *mitzvah*, an act of charity.

Typically, Madame Altman went to great pains to arrange such meetings. God had not blessed her with children. She suffered from a lassitude that bordered periodically on fits of grave depression. She had thus decided to participate as often as possible in all community events, even in the *hevra kaddishah*, the laying out of the dead.

Madame Altman had taken Edith under her wing. She found Edith a little strange, but the girl took her mind off other matters. One day she telephoned the parents:

"Ask Edith to come over for tea. And tell her to look her best."

Edith smoothed her hair, paid special attention to her eyelids and pinched her cheeks to bring colour to them. A full blouse of champagne hue, a midnight-blue velvet skirt, and she was off without even saying goodbye.

She returned home two hours later, and we were given to understand right away that he was the one, though she was incapable of relating details. By means of deduction, we concluded that he was neither handsome nor young, and that it was not at all a question of wealth. But he loved to sing, as did she (he was a cantor in a synagogue) and, above all, he was going to take her away, far away from here, to England...Mama pushed away a tear. "Are you sure you're not making a mistake?" she asked.

Edith was not listening. Her eyes shone strangely, her long hands gestured in all directions, like the wings of a bird about to take flight. Edith was going to leave us. Edith, vibrant and dreamy, our Antigone, our Cassandra...I had known it was going to happen. I found it logical, predictable, even desirable, because it had to be done. It was simply that I had trouble believing it. By what miracle would the unruly hair, the errant legs, the distant, solitary artist's eyes be able to control themselves? How could this restive and sorrowful animal submit to being caged up, tranquillized?

I felt that with her would leave a goodly measure of what I had been up to that point: the games and laughter we still shared, the poems and songs we improvised, the afternoons we spent drawing, the walks along the quays. And, far, far away, the buttercups and violets we used to pick in the country. My memory drifted all the way back,

back to the days of rolling in the grass, of picking chestnuts in the shadowy wood, back to the days of our freedom...All that had grown so pale so quickly. And tomorrow, all trace would be gone. No one would remember.

A young woman. How strange. She would be a young woman tomorrow.

And I would be left, alone with them, the two others who were growing old, the only son, the only child.

She was leaving me there, turning me over to them. The time for me was rapidly approaching, the time to stop dreaming...

Max was the son of a Polish cantor who had emigrated to England in the 1920s. After his father's death, he had assumed the same position in the same synagogue.

And he was the one Edith was going to marry...So it was impossible for us to escape the fate which, for generations, had kept us in full view of our brothers. We were forever to be their models, forever to be paid for serving as mirrors. Edith was still trying to convince herself: "In any case, I'll have an apartment in the city. I've done it, I'll have a life of my own! And then, you know, he has begun studying medicine... Of course, it's not all settled..."

She began preparing for her new role. Yet, even before the wedding, the façade started to crumble. The outbursts came one after the other, unprovoked, unpredictable.

Father rattled chairs noisily to cover her cries, and pleaded in a hushed voice:

"The neighbours! The neighbours! And the congregation, here below us. They're going to hear you. This is my undoing!"

The ceremony took place in Manchester in the presence of 350 strangers, not counting the Altmans, who had made a special trip to observe first-hand the happiness for which they were responsible. Mama wore a long, russet-red lace dress with hooded cape. I was dressed in cream-coloured gloves, glossy shoes and a navy blue suit made specially for the occasion. Papa was the most comical: in top hat and rented dinner jacket, as required by the very conventional congregation in Manchester. Edith and I, in memory of the long hours we had spent reproducing the attire of our favourite stars, had decided, as a final touch, that she would wear an exact replica of Grace Kelly's wedding gown.

While moving lightly over the synagogue's red carpet, in front of this throng of guests, I had the distinct feeling of belonging to a princely family of the cinema.

But, under the nuptial canopy, Edith's face contorted into a strange grin, then she burst into uncontrollable tears. During the rabbi's part, Max waited anxiously for her to calm down, to regain at least a measure of composure, to reduce the outburst to the touching little tear expected of a girl bidding adieu to the family nest. But the tears flowed and flowed, never stopped; and, outside, in the midday light, her face appeared distorted, swollen and red.

She came back six months later. She said there were problems, that it was hard to play her role as a respectable wife; said that it was a full-time job, an exhausting job, that she sometimes felt an irresistible urge to create a scandal...Max was ashamed. He was fearful for his position and for the child on the way. She cried, then went back home, to the front. Again I am alone, alone with the two and encircled by all the others. When I think of her, it seems that I am the only one suffering, because our suffering is identical. I keep reconstituting my little older sister's itinerary: her birth somewhere in a Transylvanian village, then, so soon afterwards, the earthquake; I picture the advances of her flight, Hungary, Austria and Germany under the last bombs, a short respite in France, and now a misty far-off shore, where, under threat of madness, she is trying so hard not to betray our ancestors.

The parents expect her to toe the mark, to renounce her troubled adolescence under the weight of responsibilities, of keeping her proper place. She is up to it, yes, they are quite sure.

I am not. I am afraid for her because I am afraid for me. Afraid I shall end up the same way. Afraid I shall never gather the strength to get out of this prison...

My mother used to say, "I forbid anyone in this household to pronounce the word "*malheur,*" misfortune.

One day when she was about to sit on one of my oil portraits, I cried out without thinking, "Watch out, *malheureuse!*"

So many nasty looks to dodge after that!...Did she ever forgive me?

"*Malchance*" or "*malchanceux,*" ill-fated, were in a sense more taboo still. It was strange that a similar word could exist in Yiddish, *shiksal,* but I rather think it is a euphemism that means something like "unlucky," a simple process of de-dramatization.

My father used to say, "One should never dramatize."

Even during the most catastrophic moments of our lives, to dare to speak of being ill-fated, we the Chosen People...

So I would draw up in my mind an account of our

impotent grudges: the grandparents I had never seen, the uncles and aunts I would never know, scarcely a few distant cousins scattered around the world.

"But it was because they were envious of us. Envy was the cause of it all!"

And, with regard to the four of us, if you please, where is the misfortune, how could we be ill-fated? The war, yes, of course, that is undeniable, but we must not take that out on God. It was not his doing, it was men and their envy.

My father used to say, "Fear God, but men — beware of men like the plague."

It is true, having known only misfortune was humiliating, after all. Whenever possible, we must act like everyone else and repeat:

"All is well, thanks be to God."

And what if evoking misfortune means inviting it in...and what if it is a mere matter of ignoring it, to the point of relegating the word to oblivion?

Besides, things had been worse. Things could always be worse.

There was really no way to counter that position, not even by asking a question, as we usually do to rekindle debate.

Things are getting better...Things are getting better and better...In the end it would all come true.

When things were going well enough, we would say: "Keyne hore" (gone the evil eye). When things began to run afoul, we would say: "*Gam zu letovah*" (it is for the best); and when things took a turn for the worse, but we could still stand up to it — it was time to revert to *"Af al pi"* (in spite of everything)

My brother-in-law, Max, at the height of the most difficult moments in his life with Edith, would trumpet like an American filmstar under contract: "Everything is aaAALL RIGHT!" And his voice, rising in a crescendo, held the *all* for a few beats, almost like a crooner, a Crosby or a Sinatra, in order to convince himself that nothing was wrong at all, not the slightest little thing...*Abi gezint.*

Abi gezint. As long as you have your health. *"Abi gezint,"* they repeated in near chorus: the rheumatics, the diabetics, the cardiacs, the arthritics of the community. *"Abi gezint,"* they bade each other after services, after having listed in minute detail their many ills — the Yiddish version of the lines the humourist Ouvrard had extracted so successfully from the woes of old age and infirmity. *"Abi gezint,"* groaned in light-hearted chortles the survivors of the camps, those who had suffered such terrible wounds and aftereffects. *"Abi gezint,"* my father said on the eve of that awful bout of peritonitis, which nearly left him dead on the operating table. *"Abi gezint, abi gezint,"* echoed my mother between liver attacks; *"Abi gezint, abi gezint,"* and the fibroma in her continued to grow, undetected. *"Abi gezint,"* my son, one should never dramatize; we do not have the right to speak of misfortune, not even of troubles, just of...minor inconveniences.

Futility. Just talk. At heart, they knew full well. They knew that their "faithfulness" to the community was responsible for the son's nervousness and for the daughter's fits of depression.

They knew, and that is why they had chased out from under our roof the words "misfortune," "ill-fated," "failure," words without hope of redress, without remedy, for even if we were incurable, condemned, we could still look each other in the whites of our eyes and say, "*Gam zu letovah,*" it is for the best.

And even when everything was falling apart, coming undone, we still had "*Af al pi,*" in spite of everything...

"**D**aniel! Daniel!" drivelled the old rabbi at the *heder*. "Daniel! *Du herst nisht!* You never listen...*Kenstu unz nisht makhn a bisele nakhes*...Are you never going to give your teachers and your parents a little *nakhes*?"

"*Nakhes*," almost untranslatable, covering so many notions...*Nakhes*: if the children conducted themselves as good, pious Jews, if they could be counted on to recite the Kaddish when you were gone. *Nakhes*: if they married an authentic *Yiddish kin*. *Nakhes:* if they reared their own children in the age-old tradition. *Nakhes:* if they succeeded in landing a good and proper job.

The children...Always the children. Always. And even when the children had completed the entire program, at the least suggestion of ill health, the parents were distressed for us, certainly, but it is fact that they also felt they had not received the complete satisfaction from us that comes from no shortfall of *nakhes*.

I thought about Edith. What incredible task had she not undertaken in order to give the parents their *nakhes?* The marriage to a true man of religion, the baby who would soon be learning Hebrew, the status she was trying so desperately to maintain...Alas, madness seized her periodically: the terrible nervous depressions that descended upon her for a month, then two, then three months running, the improprieties she uttered or committed then; all that — everything she had not been able to shoulder, try as she might, since, as a small child, she had run from one bombing to the next, from one shelter to the next — all that excluded her from the list of those capable of giving *nakhes.*

From that I drew my lesson: no sense in beating my head against the wall. It was a lost cause from the start. First my tardiness at services, and now my desertions. But even without them, not a chance, they had read it in my face, in my eyes: it was hopeless, irreparable.

That is why my parents were disconsolate when it came to *nakhes.* Since I could never make it up to them, I looked for ways, every way, to create my own *nakhes.* I was aware that this urge stemmed from some sort of perverted egotism. I was following a path quite different from Edith's. It was clear, perfectly obvious. I had chosen to circumvent, to dodge, to avoid, whereas she had moved steadily forward, despite the adversity, from her earliest childhood, never allowing herself to let her guard down.

After Edith's departure, I moved into the space at the

extreme end of the Talmud Torah hall on the third floor. My sister had rearranged the old attic as best she could. It was good to "get away," to enjoy spending at least a few hours no longer under the watchful eyes of the others. Edith had left behind a number of old books, classics, a Koran among volumes by Colette, Camus, and Marcel Aymé. The window looked onto a courtyard from which rose, during the day, the comforting sounds of a workshop. It was a novel thing for me to have a window opening onto the normal, soothing, workaday world. It was good finally to have a grasp of this country...On the one side, the books of a municipal library; on the other, the bustle of a workshop. I settled in amongst my books and notebooks. I was about to begin my sixth year at school and, as Edith had in that year, I would have to start sorting through that gigantic jumble known as literature. During the preceding summer, I devoured, indiscriminately and without digesting very well, the volumes I had inherited from Edith's aborted studies. A new world was born...The problem with my new room was that, in coming and going, I had to cross the long room that adjoined it, where there was always a crowd of people either studying or meeting for discussion; there, too, another world took form, noisy and smoke-laden, that of a wedding or a *bar mitzvah*, a world into which I was compelled to immerse myself, like it or not.

In the evening, however, the building was deserted and within its sombre vastness I felt a little too removed from my parents, whose vague presence I discerned by the light from their apartment that filtered down into the abyss separating us.

An abyss. At night the synagogue became a fearful, mute precipice...Sometimes, in the silence, a creak, and then another, and then many others echoing into the depths: probably a vagrant who had escaped the sexton's watchful eye and was stretching out between the columns to spend the night, only to be startled awake by Rav Nussan's voice when *shachrit* began the following morning. Opposite me, on the other side of the courtyard, France lay asleep: complete silence covered the workshops and the offices.

A good Jew always gets up before everyone else for *shachrit*, and my room was already vibrating from the first recitations.

I must have been dreaming. France did not exist.

At regular intervals, we disappeared into the sanctimonious entryway of the *préfecture*, across from the impassive Cathedral of Notre Dame.

Everything was so precarious. Everything could be questioned, undone.

"Papers," someone would say, "let us have your papers! Don't you understand French?"

A good question. In those days, Mama and Papa still understood quite poorly the most beautiful language of the most beautiful country in the world. And it was not by chance that they came to be counted there, to renew their residence permit.

They nudged me ahead of them so that I might interpret.

"What do you want?"

My father and I had removed our headgear in order to look like everyone else, and, from the window, the clerk was able to see only my hair — still the fair hair of a child.

"Our residence permit...We've come to renew it."

"Why didn't you say so? Papers!"

Beside himself, my father tried to find them in his vest pocket for what seemed an eternity. The people in the endless line behind us grew impatient: the Italians, the Spanish, the Algerians...

"Madame, born in Deb...reuh...euh...re...recen? Debrecen. Is that it?"

She exaggerated the difficulty of deciphering the name and, in so doing, made my mother ashamed to have been born.

"And you, Monsieur, in Bé...Béjus."

She got it almost at once. So the fat clerk, when she was a fat little girl, must have studied Latin.

"*Apatride*," stateless. She scribbled out a form which she handed to the dark-grey rodent next to her.

"You! You! Wait on the bench over there. You'll be called."

An hour later, the "*apatrides*" left and restored their spirits along the banks of the Seine..."*Apatrides, apatrides,*" squealed the seagulls.

Later, we had the right to be labelled refugees: "Romanian refugees." The officials here always put up that same haughty façade. But it was here, nonetheless, in France, a country of welcome, that all the stateless people of the world came together. The proof of it was all those spectres who lined up from the quays to the *préfecture* in order to document their existence.

One day I had had enough of it, enough of it for all of us, of being treated like an indigent and illiterate foreigner fresh off the boat from the colonies. I told myself: they may not have even finished primary school and here I am, devouring Molière, Hugo, Balzac, Prévert...

She was a skinny thing in glasses, with lips painted in the form of a képi, a gendarme cap, heavily on the upper lip and lightly on the lower one. As usual, my father nudged me ahead in line.

I had grown taller. In a turtleneck and jeans, with my pale eyes, I looked much more French than the rest of us. Or so we thought.

"You, if you please, with parents: state nationality or country of origin, leave papers, sit down and wait!"

"I beg your pardon."

"You. Papers. Give. After. Will call."

My father nudged me with his elbow: what does he think I'm up to all of a sudden? Let's get this over with. He'd understood her words immediately, hours ago it seems. Had I become an idiot?

No, father. I have just decided to have a little fun, to play the ass until I can get even with them. Fortunately, in those days, the voice-amplifier did not yet exist, and we could talk to them at the window while looking them straight in the eye. I counted off a ten-second silence, and then I articulated, indeed declaimed, loudly and clearly, for us and for all the others who had been waiting for hours:

"I beg your pardon, Madame. I believe I have quite understood the essence of your utterance. However, the substance of your instructions seems to be quite lacking in clarity. Could it be that you find it difficult to express yourself properly in French?"

As the *képi* of her lips became even more pronounced, several *apatrides* laughed and sneered and applauded behind us. Of course my poor parents now expected the worst, to be detained in the *Conciergerie* and, why not, God forbid, to be deported, sent back to Transylvania. They looked at me with blaming eyes, eyes full of worry and rancour. Never mind that we had not had to wait nearly so long this time, and that she had been very careful not to distort our names.

*Apatride...Refugee...*Father had had a bellyfull of it. Never had he succeeded in establishing a nationality, something solid, a paper that admitted its owner to the ranks of those entitled to live on this earth. A NATIONALITY, a legitimate place in the sun. He had been born in Transylvania in the days of the Austrian Empire, under the quivering iron fist of the aging Franz Josef. Then came the first Great War, and the country did not resist the Romanians. So the people there had been Austrian, Hungarian, Romanian, Romanian, Hungarian, according to the whims of history. Not unlike Alsace-Lorraine, one might say. As time went by, only the word "Jew" remained to differentiate their papers from all the others. Ultimately, it was probably the most accurate designation, but it was not a nationality, it was just a seal that resembled a star. Then came 1948, the miracle awaited for centuries, which made every Jew, automatically, an Israeli — if he was willing to build the country...

Nationality: Israeli, the right to travel everywhere,

head high, the right to wage war, the right to vote or not to vote, the right to become angry, even to protest and demonstrate.

But poor, frail Rozsa did not have it in her. Her dream had sprung up here, and she slowly took root in this country, where steak and chocolate were available. Paris helped her. Paris, its lights, its boutiques and its frivolities. Paris took her mind off other things, helped her forget at least momentarily her own once large family: her father, her mother, her little brothers and sisters who had remained in Hungary only to be shipped off to be gassed, just yesterday...No, impossible, impossible to envy her sole surviving brother, who had escaped in order to set things right and had set off again to another front, to face other enemies, beneath the fiery sun of the Middle East.

Well, then, since that was the way it was, *ein breirah*, no choice, another solution had to be found. But "Romanian refugee," the words stuck tearfully in my father's throat. They must have sounded just as painful to him as *büdös Zsidó*, dirty Jew.

And why not become French, after all? On a passport it was a declaration of pride: NATIONALITÉ FRANÇAISE.

"And then, with that," he said, "we can go anywhere. We'll be respected."

Yes. Go for "French nationality." He would gallicize his name: no more Yohanan or Janos; he would be Jean. And my mother, Rose. Frankly, Jean, Rose and Daniel Jonasz, it would go completely unnoticed, would it not?

Except, to do it, we would have to take exams. A series

of interviews at the same *préfecture,* and then...I never quite knew what else. I was too young for my own French birth to carry any weight. But it might be helpful, it just might. And later, when I turned sixteen it would be automatic, because I would simply have to choose, to exercise my legal option, and then my parents' file would follow as a matter of course.

How impatient he was. He could not stand the waiting. Alas, after each step of the procedure, the heavy cloud of failure lay ominously above them. Another long wait, and for nothing. The Caesar of naturalization had turned thumbs down.

"Sorry, Monsieur Jonasz, you're not quite there yet. You don't seem...integrated enough. It's surely the profession, a very unusual one, in which you're engaged: secretary of a synagogue, outside of French society, outside of our nation. I don't blame you for it. Look, everyone does what he can...with what he has. Only you have not become assimilated enough, you understand..."

"*Vey, Monsieur l'inspecteur,*" he exhaled in a sigh.

"*Igen, Igen,* Monsieur," my mother added in Hungarian: emotion made her commit the worst of blunders.

Not assimilated enough. In the synagogue, an assimilated Jew was known as a traitor, a renegade, a worthless man, but for that man behind the desk, assimilation was the supreme virtue, the Open Sesame of legitimacy...Come, now..."*Oy vey! S'iz shver tsu zayn a Yid!*" Oh Misery! How hard it is to be a Jew! What did people have against him, anyway? He dressed like everyone else. He had not let his beard or his side-curls grow. He even removed his hat when necessary. He had blue eyes, light brown hair, so many French people seemed more foreign than he.

No, decidedly, nothing would ever change. The Jews would always be hated, that was all there was to it. And, undeniably, his profession did not help matters. Nor did his accent, which meant sure failure in his citizenship interviews. He knew it was best to say as little as possible: "Even an ignorant man who remains silent can pass for a sage," it is written...So he took it out on her:

"You numbskull, you could at least go five short minutes without speaking Hungarian when we're being interviewed!"

"I was too tired today... Next time, next time, Janos, I promise..."

This time they had really done everything right. They had carefully checked their appearance in the mirror before leaving. What difference was there between them and the people in *Papa, Maman, la bonne et moi*, the André Luguet–Gaby Morlay couple? Their French was appreciably better now, and he had forewarned her about punctuating her sentences with the Yiddish expressions she used to ward off the ever-present evil eye: "My son works very hard at school, *keyne hore...*"

That particular day, they emerged light-hearted from the Métro station Cité, across from the flower market.

Then she even remained completely silent for two long hours in the waiting room.

But at the crucial moment, following a question addressed to her, she turned to her husband and, in a panicked voice, asked, "Do you understand, do you understand what he's asking?"

Alas, alas, she had said it in Hungarian.

The Jewish *lycée* lay hidden amidst the plane trees and the chestnut trees deep within the recesses of its well-shaded grounds. It had been a private estate. The layout of its classrooms and offices, its dining halls and corridors, was therefore strangely unconventional.

The first time I walked down the narrow, low-ceilinged hallway leading to the director's oak office door, I sensed a surge from out of the distant past, a momentary return to the days of my childhood and the improvised classrooms which overlooked our front steps in the country...The door opened. I was greeted by a giant, and it took quite some time for my gaze to inch up and meet his: two large, algae-green beacons concentrating steadily on me. A young doctor of theology, he was also a hero of the Resistance. A *maquis*, a word which smelled of thyme, of brushwood, of freedom. *Maquis*, like Monsieur Seguin's nanny goat, he had left the safety of the pasture, had done battle with the wolf and had not been eaten...

Everyone, boys and girls alike, loved him. He was the father, the fantasized brother for whom there was no model in our families. His tall stature, the perfect proportions of his sculpted face and his full mouth, his wide, light, oriental-shaped eyes, all that did not stem from physical beauty alone, but rather from divine recompense for his enormous learning, for his mysticism and his conversations with God. (Had Moses not been visited by a strange, resplendent beauty as he descended the slopes of Mount Sinai?)

In truth, I no longer believed any of that. I did not believe that anyone could have even the most inconsequential of conversations with any god. God was always mute. He had nothing to say to anybody. He had been quite content, throughout the ages, to bring down upon us cataclysm after cataclysm. But Sacha, irresistibly drawn to the Kabbala and numerology, Sacha, possessed by chimæra, visions, incarnated wondrously the possible prophet — if it is true that prophets existed...

The Jewish *lycée*, the synagogue, the synagogue, the Jewish *lycée*. At least things were clear now. No one would need to ask why I was a dissident among my people, why I was so different and why I was a stranger to the others. Line number nine from the Bonne-Nouvelle station to the Porte Saint-Cloud station shuttled me daily from the old people's ghetto to the ghetto of the youth, round trip. I had only thirty-five minutes, eighteen stops each way, to take in what had till now been closed to me: Paris. I was fascinated by the brief incursions into goy country...It was rush hour, they were all there: the young businessmen in three-piece suits, briefcases in hand; the young lovers who took advantage of the crowded conditions to kiss and fondle each other before running off to their respective jobs, the elderly labourers whose heads dipped with drowsiness into the folds of their tabloids, *L'Equipe* or *Paris-Jour*, the working girls, many of them pregnant, who never tired of knitting — blue-white-pink — and who, after the baby had been born, devoured photo-novels by the score. During our seven years on the same, unchanging métro line, we came to recognize one another, without ever exchanging a word. Nor did we cease scrutinizing each other to determine how the other was doing, whether the other was prospering or falling into decline.

I admired these young women on their way to work at dawn: their fastidious, almost ascetic concern for their appearance, their hair and their makeup. My mother liked to repeat:

"Lower-class working girls, middle-class girls, millionaires, in Paris you can hardly tell the difference. Always impeccable, no matter the hour, like gaily wrapped candies fresh from the box, and so slim, so slim!..."

It is true: those forced labourers in petticoats I saw on my morning treks across and beneath the city were indeed exquisite. Thanks to them, over the years, I discovered in sequence the various dictates of fashion. Huddled together like that, like so many asparagus stalks,

there were first the Bardot types with "sauerkraut" hair —
somewhat stringy and delicately teased out of place — and
heavy eyeliner reaching back to the temples. One
autumn, the eyeliner had receded mysteriously to a point
one or two millimetres from the outer edge of the eyelid,
the hair had grown suddenly shorter, and the only thing
these Sylvie Vartan types lacked was her toothy
grin...Toward the end, still blonde, the smooth, little-girl-
model strands cascaded down to their shoulders and
were held in place by a headband. Everything appeared
washed out, thick eyebrows or white lips. They began to
seek a hollowing effect, to accentuate all the places where
shadows might hide: the temples, the cheekbones, the
brow ridges, and soon the Demoiselles de Rochefort
(Catherine Deneuve and Françoise Dorléac) had the joy
of announcing the birth of several thousand brand-new
little sisters...Sometimes, perched on a flap-seat, a broke
and overly made-up walk-on actress on her way to the
Boulogne Studios saw the cinema posters that lined the
walls of each station and dreamed that Truffaut was waiting for her alone to exchange a stolen kiss with Antoine
Doinel.

Already. The number 72 bus at the Rhin-et-Danube
stop...I had regrouped my forces only to have to do combat of another sort — with the vulgar razzing and hazing
perpetrated on us by our Sephardic brothers from North
Africa. They had multiplied and we, the Ashkenazi, had
become their Jews. They poked fun at our mannered

accents and our taste for literature and the arts. To them,
we were "snobs" and "fags"...We kept our distance, therefore, unsure of how we might be able to live alongside
these prank-loving Mediterranean cousins who, like the
goys, paid no heed to our fragile sensibilities and our
great misfortunes. Auschwitz? A war? A massacre somewhere back in history...So remote, all that,...Auschwitz,
Maidanek, Treblinka, impossible words. Nordic syllables.
The geography of the far reaches of the earth, enshroud-
ed in mist. Unimaginable under the blue skies of Tipasa
or Carthage.

Their imposing voices resounded in the classroom.
They called out boisterously to each other, insulted each
other, all in Arabic. And we didn't even use Yiddish to
respond in kind. It seemed that we could no longer pronounce it: I think we had become ashamed of it...

They followed the same precepts that we did, but in an
entirely different manner. And, above all, they knew how
to laugh, to really laugh, without feeling obliged, as we
did, to make witticisms. The coarsest of jokes seemed to
burst forth spontaneously, without the least taboo, and,
despite their recent uprooting, they enjoyed a true adolescence and even took pleasure in evoking and exhibit-
ing the phallic god Zob.

Yet, among the Ashkenazi, I also found unsuspected
differences. There had always been Jews in France, for
generations: the Weills, the Dreyfuses, the Blochs, who
lived on avenue Mozart. It was practically impossible to
penetrate their circle. They respected the majority of the
rites but, somewhat like the practice in the United States,

the main thing was to belong to a congregation. They fulfilled their religious obligations at the Copernic or Montevideo synagogues in the sixteenth arrondissement where everyone spoke French. Their services resembled ours, but whether they kneeled to light a candle or kissed the Torah, each movement was reduced to pure gesture: controlled, conventional, aseptic, cleansed of the mediaeval primitivism of the *shtetl.*

There were, of course, rich people among the Weills, the Dreyfuses, the Blochs. They had attained the peace of mind of those who owned and would always own real estate in Paris or in the provinces, as well as at least a small permanent collection of artistic masterpieces. They sometimes indulged in the luxury of squandering vast sums on absurd financial deals, thus proving that they were indeed true "Franzos." For all of that, they were never to be refused entry to the Great Synagogue alongside the Rothschilds (distant cousins) on the Great Day of Reckoning. A sexton in a cocked hat and wearing a uniform dating from the time of Napoleon, founder of the Israelite Consistory of France, would surely usher them to their appointed places...Short of money? They would simply have to get by without servants. Michel's parents had decided to cut down on their protein intake, but they would keep the maid. Appearances were saved. Madame Weber could continue to sound the hand bell, peremptorily and with a refined gesture as in the past, and, as in the past, Mélanie would come running with a silver platter—except that, more and more frequently—it would contain...noodles.

The French Jews—excuse me—Israelites...I envied their certainty of being at home here. What had happened, from their point of view, in the 1940s? They had refused to believe it, right up to the end. After all, they had served France for generations...But even they, in the end, had been sought out, and found...They would not talk about it. They, too, must have been ashamed. Not for having believed in France. But for having been deceived by her, good Frenchmen that they were.

Besides, had things not returned to normal? The children were growing up in the good old Franco-Judaic tradition: synagogue on Saturday, scouts on Sunday with the Israelite Scouts of France, skiing and other winter sports at Zermatt...And, should the culture and learning of our ancestors be slipping imperceptibly away: Jewish school for the children and grand *bar mitzvahs* in the presence of Chief Rabbi Kaplan...It was a means of protecting themselves against the fanatical Zionism that threatened to transform their future professors of medicine into manure-gathering wretches in a kibbutz. They also had to protect themselves against that other fanaticism, the religious fanaticism brought to France by the survivors of Central Europe; and, indeed, the little Blochs and Dreyfuses and Weills were very curious to come home with me to see what a truly Jewish family was like, real survivors, real practising Jews...In exchange for which I could expect a lone invitation, tea and *petits-beurre* in the living rooms of their palatial apartments.

The *lycée* let us out Fridays at noon, and each of us left for his own particular *Shabbat.*

The seventh day, the day of rest...Nothing was more exhausting than the racket that shook the entire building on Friday afternoons; nothing was bleaker than the ecstasy that was supposed to come over us with the sounding of the fateful hour, brutally snuffing out everything that kept us going the rest of the week.

The *erev Shabbat* service marked the last formal activity before the heavy cloak of imposed idleness pressed its full weight upon me...The last kaddish...The men of the congregation filed out slowly, followed by their wives, who appeared to have renounced their handbags—forbidden objects on this holy day.

We went upstairs to eat. On the clean, fresh tablecloth, my mother had placed the braided bread and had covered it with the richly embroidered crimson velvet that she had taken such care to protect during her many wanderings.

With nightfall, Queen *Shabbat* delivered us over to the interference and static, to the muffled sneers and short shrill cries that kept the three of us glued to the telephone receiver. The voice surged, cavernous and nasal:

"Ah, well you haven't all been fried yet, have you? It's a hardy race, that one! But you needn't bother yourselves about it. Not in the least! We'll take care of you. We know where you're holed up. We'll blow the place up!"

Father and I laughed loudly to reassure Mama. She was already whimpering with panic.

"What do you expect, my dear Rozsa?...It's always been like that...As long as it's only on the telephone..."

The candles began to flicker. It was bedtime. I remained a few moments to breathe in the acrid perfume rising from the snuffed flames. Soon everything was pitch black.

I started back down to my room. It was forbidden to touch the time-controlled light switch, but I knew the steps by heart. At the seventh step, through a small pane of glass, I could see distinctly the luxurious apartment building across the street. There, the lights still shone brightly and, through the fine window sheers, I could make out sparkling chandeliers, the bluish hue of a television, figures dancing. For them, our neighbours, it was the weekend...

Hidden there in the darkness, I waited. Through the uncurtained window of the concierges' quarters, I was often able to witness the methodical striptease of a heavy-set brunette who, after having sprayed herself with some nondescript toilet water, slipped into a large, soft bed with her dog. Then the husband dashed into view. He was short, white-skinned and completely undressed...His penis jolted about as he pounced on her; the dog scampered away just before the light went out. There was nothing more to see.

I went down a few steps farther to turn and grope my way through the long, intense darkness leading to my room.

All the while, Mama had been unable to sleep. The *Shabbat* was always cause for apprehension, as was any reception. It was forbidden to forget anything. And there was always the danger of fire. On the *Shabbat*, no source of energy whatsoever could be activated. She had therefore lighted the gas range before nightfall in order to be able to serve us hot meals. That night, she would get up at all hours, hounded by the fear of a gas leak or a fire. Devices to regulate such things did exist, but it seemed that only the *bourgeoises* of the community had a right to them. After all, generations of good Jewish wives had followed the same routine...

The next day, interminable prayers were said, one after the other, bringing increasing numbers to the synagogue. Then there was a large *kiddush*: schnapps, cointreau, *leykekh*, mochas and sometimes even a colossal *tshulent* that Mama had let simmer all night. For our father, it was a day for friends, good food and studying the Holy Scriptures, just as it had been when he was a student at the *yeshivah*.

I would have preferred to delve into a history book,

but there he was already coming toward me with the *Pirkei Avot*, the precepts of our ancestors. I would have liked to go to the cinema, too, but to touch money on the sabbath was a grave sin. The same for going to the Bois de Boulogne, because that entailed taking a bus, or for petting the cat, because on *Shabbat* even he became impure.

I ran outside toward the street, stopping at the edge of the crossing. Perhaps I would see a friend passing by...I persisted, full of boredom and hope. I paced from one sidewalk to the other absurdly waiting to recognize a face. I went up and down in search of someone to help me fill my Saturday afternoons. I waited and watched all the busy people, some with armfuls of packages, others on their way to shops, restaurants or the cinema, all of them allowed the temptations of the city. Another world.

I returned disappointed. Mama had spread out a Hungarian newspaper on the table. And absent-mindedly she began to sing softly "*Szomoru vasarnap*": "Sombre Sunday," in Hungarian. And ever since I have always felt a sadness on the Shabbat and later on Sundays, too, and on every other day marked by inactivity, when time has to be killed. She smiled at me absent-mindedly. Her face was that of an old little girl whose tangles were teased indelicately out of place...Her ivory complexion and her colourless lips (makeup was forbidden) frightened me a little. I took flight again, back out to the sidewalk.

"What are you waiting there for, my poor little friend?

Why not come join us for *motsei Shabbat,* the closing of *Shabbat,* the Queen?"

A painfully understanding expression appears beneath Monsieur Klein's black felt hat. He nudges me gently. I follow obediently. *motsei Shabbat.* Above us Mama chanted:

"*A gite vokh, a gite vokh,*" a good week, a good week to all.

A gite vokh. It is finally over. Now I can begin to live again.

It was hot under the chestnut trees in the small square, and the coolness of the movie theatre was tempting. But on that day our class was not going to see a film for entertainment or adventure. We were being taken there for instructional purposes: a program consisting of a recent documentary on the Genocide, taken from records filmed by the Nazis in the ghettos and concentration camps.

There were many among us who knew little about it, almost nothing. I thought I knew. I was born of the survivors; they had told me everything, and I had remembered, retained it all. I had only come along to accompany my classmates.

Everything began as usual: the half-light of an old neighbourhood movie house during the sultry days of late spring; the Movietone newsreel; the ushers who passed up and down the aisles with their irresistible fare, chocolates and caramels and cool, refreshing *esquimaux* on a stick. Then a short on the marvels of the newly restored Château de Versailles.

Now the feature. Commentary by Léon Zitrone, who had done features on Princess Margaret, Princess Grace of Monaco, and Paola de Liège. He could not be too frightening.

But this time I did not even recognize his voice, from which all pomposity, all reassurance had disappeared. And the scenes that appeared on the screen, I did not recognize them either, none of them...Scenes in which the dead stirred to life in an awesome spectacular: a cast of six million for the most fantastic, the most incredible, the most demented story every told.

> Warsaw first first the ghetto
> Smiles come hard but they come
> They do not know
> Packed in there by the dozens
>   into shanty houses
> A girl cleanses the lice from her brother
> She looks like Edith
> Like her, she dreams of lace,
>   of a glorious wedding, of richly
>   embroidered cloths for the table
>
> But winter has set in and with it famine
> Outside, paving stones powdered with snow
>   and on them women, old men, children
>   strip clean the bones of a dead horse
>
> Kilometres to the south and west
>   the Führer
> In closeup from the rear in Nuremberg Stadium
>   before the endless masses (all that remains

of humanity no doubt)
Voluntary concentration
Hundreds of thousands of howling heroes

Now it is time for a train ride
   the express to Auschwitz-Birkenau
But where oh where are the children
   of so short a time ago
Dead of hunger
Dragged to a common grave
Monstrous foetuses
Heads as large as torsos
   bouncing and bumping in the wheelbarrow
The film is silent but I hear the bong bong
   their skulls their rigid broken limbs
   beat against the metal

And now a Mengele selection
A nervous cameraman
The pictures quiver black grey black
   and ashen or else it is my eyes misting over

Already typhus
Faces heads of the living dead
The mouth a gaping hole hungering
   for a last morsel of life

Black butterflies flit across a distorted screen
Old films worn by use
No. No. Scarcely fifteen years. My age soon
It is my eyes trying to turn away.
   for if I wish I can clearly detect
   the nudity the bodies the tibias the marionettes
   nude as they cannot be in life
Detect the zebra stripes of
   ribs long and charred of shadow
   and hair of underarm and pubis

And on these skeletal mounds now appear
    only the black tufts of vegetation
    the penises beneath
    lifelines long and useless
    yet whole and fleshy upon their frame
    of fleshless bone

To the ovens now
    the skylights crackle
    flames light the theatre

A grandmother bent or hunched
    gathering her pack
    gathering her two grandchildren
    heading toward the open space
    before the shower house

Inside women await the water
    round and smooth of body
    The water does not come
Waiting to be photographed
    by some apprentice Renoir
    at death's door

Arrays of booty
Gold teeth selected and weighed
    upon long wooden tables
Dolls in an open shed seated and quiet as mice
    miniature witnesses mute and orphaned
    of their young mothers
Strands of hair to fill the mattresses
Eyeglasses vertiginous and fragile
    pyramids of small metallic circles
    indispensable for sight
    never having had the time to see

Already the war's end

Time passes quickly on the screen
The Germans panic
   they know the end is near
Nothing must remain
Everyone must go
Not enough room in ovens too small

The cameraman has stopped filming

The GI's take their place
Flickering silhouettes of soldiers
   climbing over mountains of cadavers
   hundreds of thousands waiting
   decomposing in the mud
   spattered by the drizzle
Closeup of the white of bones piercing skin
   closeup of blackened sockets
   and of mouths
   still mutely shouting their hunger
   their pain
   their fear
   their error in trusting too much
   the might of the Almighty
   and not enough in the Führer's

Lights.

It is over. My classmates begin to stir to life. It is so hot in the theatre. Now, before filing out, they ask for another ice-cream. Our chaperones are grave, but there is no mistake about it. They display the serious satisfaction of teachers who have conducted an excellent class. A syllabus followed to the letter.

"Well, Daniel, are you going to stay there and take root?"

Outside, even the chestnut trees are unable to screen out the blast of May heat.

113

So I did not know after all. I had not seen anything. I who never tire of pictures, a glutton for films, I have been caught in my own trap. I thought I believed in nothing but pictures. And now I had to find out that with the same camera that filmed the little dark-haired girl with the sapphire eyes and the dog named Lassie, the two of them too beautiful to be true, it was possible, on this side of the Atlantic, to film during the same period that incredible evil story with grimacing actors too atrocious not to be true.

Out of the same desperation that brings a defiant no to the lips of those visited by a sudden sorrow, I threw myself into my mother's arms, blessed her for telling me not to worry, for saying it could never happen again, blessed her for having all her hair, for being stout of body, for the soft youthfulness of her skin unmarked by blue-black numbers...But her reassurances were empty words and gestures; for in her arms I understood what all who had made it through that ordeal were saying: no one could ever know, no one could ever bear witness. Even those who had lived it, because it was impossible.

I had been plunged into a fit of madness by a procession of mute shades upon a flat screen, but I would never know more than a pallid version bordering on falsehood. I had never heard the screams. I had never been hunted down. I had been spared the hunger, the terror, the supplications in the freezing cold, the disease, the odour of smouldering human flesh.

From below, minha prayers echoed up to where I was. They were singing His praise. I wanted them to scream bloody murder.

So they had forgiven Him. So they had forgotten Them. I would be ready, henceforth, watchful and ready to screen out their faith and their praise. Neither would penetrate the sanctuary of my room. The *Shmoneh Esrei*, their eighteen benedictions, would not gain entry. God, if he existed, had no right whatsoever to even the most insignificant sign of reverence.

And mankind? It was time to stop playing games. I knew that I could not not choose sides. Others had chosen for me...before my birth.

A new distaste for the outside world came over me, for that monster with thousands of eyes to seek you out, with thousands of voices to denounce you, with thousands of arms to pack you into railroad cars.

The Paris Metro. I am going to the swimming pool with Claude.

The Paris Metro. Gare de l'Est. How to cope with the thought: the subway for rounding us up, the train station for shipping us off? Not to mention it. Claude and I are going swimming. We are seated facing each other, making light of the posters. A robust woman in her fifties is staring at us. I know exactly what she is thinking: I am fifty years old and I reckon one of those young rascals ought to give me his seat so I can sit down. Claude has no idea any of this is happening. He continues his joking.

The woman nudges closer, so close in fact that one of her fat thighs pushes against my arm. She is gaining ground, staring all the while. I stare back at her, eyeball to eyeball. It is not easy. It is contrary to everything I have been taught, but I have to do it. I have to.

In the Paris Metro in 1960, a child simply cannot give up his seat to an adult. Cannot. What was this woman doing twenty years ago? Was she concerned whether or not some old Jews had a place to sit in railroad cars sealed shut and bursting at the seams?

In 1960, in the Paris Metro, only a child has the right to a seat.

Paris, 1960, where I had agreed to live as though in Sighet in 1880. I still did not speak Yiddish. Yiddish, a language for corpses, never crossed my lips; but I felt its every nuance, distinguished every variation of accent, was able to localize the origins of every speaker..

The circle had closed tight around me. Suddenly. So soon. And now in no time at all I had rejected the world and all its vastness. Like Edith. No, sooner still than she.

Mad. I was going mad, as mad as Edith. If the process had been retarded at all, it was simply because I had been born in another setting, sunny and welcoming, because I had learned to walk accompanied by my dog and my hen, because my playground had been a vast meadow and the nearby wood.

As for mankind, it had taken Paris, Paris and the Metro, for me to recognize the carnivorous gleam in its eyes. Mad. I was going as mad as everyone else. But given the monstrous madness that had so recently overcome

Europe, that unacceptable madness, no other choice lay open to me.

So be it. No further need to live adrift between two worlds, no further need for those incessant justifications. So be it. Too tiring. Too complicated. My life was going to become simple. It was simply a matter of going along with things, with the Jewish *lycée*, with the synagogue, with everything. And also with the madness I now shared with my father and Mama. I was finally going to put their lessons to good use, to give them their measure of *nakhes*.

The film had brought things back into focus, and all of a sudden my fear had subsided: this small community, this exact and touching reproduction of the one my father had known, and my grandfather, too, and so many others before them, would protect me by separating me from that other world. Why try to escape? Where would I go?

Here nothing had changed. The survivors were few, but they had managed to bring with them, intact, the odours from back there, the sounds and the rites from before. Yiddish, the *kiddush*, *Talmud Torah*, they were all victories over the atrocious and ever-present past. And even if I continued being stifled by it, smothered, I owed them at least that, I owed it to those who had lived, truly lived, every frame of the film that had inscribed itself with such minute precision upon my nightly reel of nightmares.

They had returned, the survivors, orphaned and

widowed of spouses and children, they had returned to warm and comfort themselves, because nothing had changed here, returned to relive that other past, because no one could understand them anywhere else.

Nothing had changed except the forearms marked by blue-black numbers. I never tired of studying their faces, of reading them. I made charcoal sketches of them, which I tacked to the walls of my room, next to the photos of my favourite actresses. My two worlds merged there, and the more fantastic of the two was without question the one I was living day after day.

They had returned...Those who talked about it revolted me because it seemed to me that Auschwitz was beyond words.

Those who did not talk about it revolted me, too, those who tried to go on with their lives as though nothing had happened. All of them wanted me to live their memories; they wanted me to become the child they had been, to belong to a past which no longer existed except as a dramatization, a theatre set.

Some of them had turned away from God. The Dachau cancer continued its painful rampage within their stomachs and entrails. The rage, the bitter rancour remained unabated. They still knew how to hate and dreamed of slitting throats—Hess, for example, who was paying the exorbitant price of pining away in his cell, or of dismembering Mengele, who at that very moment was probably taking a morning dip in his swimming pool ensconced in the depths of the Uruguayan jungle. They even regretted Hitler's decision to take his own life; but, after all, there was no real proof, perhaps he was still alive...Then Wiesenthal would find him, and they would have to find a way to execute him six million times before finishing him off.

Yom Kippur. The Goldbergs observed the occasion by indulging in a regal feast. Yes. They chose that very day of sacred fasting to stuff themselves to the gills. And where did they do it when the weather permitted? Outside, on the restaurant terrace just across from the synagogue where they sat down with a blissful sigh before a sumptuous *choucroute garnie*: sauerkraut and pork. That is how they provoked and challenged their God and all those who believed they were made in his image. God. They had no intention of remembering him. But men. Impossible to forget them. They had lived so closely with them. They remembered everything and everyone: the sadism and apathy of some, the torn flesh and hunger of others, and especially their own hunger. That is why the Goldbergs chose *Yom Kippur* to fill their gullets to the brim.

Across the way, the practising Jews were filing out onto the opposite sidewalk fresh from services, their eyes gleaming with religious fervour. In the evening, they would sit down to their *café au lait* and cake. The young sprouts had taken root here; weddings were becoming more and more frequent. People even began dancing at them, as before. The candles lit for the dead continued to gutter in the depths of the synagogue, but people still tried to forget—it was only natural. Some who had lived that terrible experience even insisted they felt no hatred. Hatred. I don't know what it is any more, they would say. Besides, I never really felt it. Yes. There were those who insisted that they had never felt it at all, that at no moment did they ever stop believing in God, that never had they ceased observing the rites as faithfully as circumstances permitted, that they had awaited and continued to await the Messiah.

Friedman was different from the others. He taught Hebrew and never tired of having us read the story of Agnon's goat, that wonderful creature who could guide its followers to the Promised Land, even from far-off Russia, because it had discovered a magical grotto, a fabulous shortcut, a Zionist express tunnel! He had not seen the mythical animal himself, but he had encountered other incredible creatures, monstrous ones...at Auschwitz. It was there, people said, that he contracted the terrible tic that caused his facial muscles to go into spasm every thirty seconds or so. Our young Sephardic brothers from North Africa laughed openly and to the point of delirium during solemn events — commemorations and awards ceremonies — when that deathly grin contorted his face suddenly and broke the serious spell the voice of our prestigious Sacha had cast. In any event, Friedman was elsewhere, forever at watch before the flames he had seen consume his entire family. Between two of Bialik's poetic phrases, when he found the joking too harsh to withstand, that terrible grin would come over him and then he would stage for us an unbearable scene filled with victims and executioners. Friedman bulged his eyes from their sockets in pantomime of those who were strangled, shrivelled himself up like a prune in imitation of those constricted by dysentery. Friedman. An awesome comedian who succeeded in depicting the colossal bestiality of SS troops. Before long, his face and his body, both so fantastically, so atrociously expressive, turned our nervous laughter into a deadly silence. Then his voice would rise:

"I know you. I know all men...They stink...All humanity stinks..."

People spend their lives accumulating large quantities of objects, as though to protect themselves, to barricade themselves and their bodies, so nude and so fragile, from the world. All those objects for which men have killed since the beginning of time, killed to acquire, killed to retain. All those objects which serve to place others on their guard, to keep them out. But deep inside of us, there is always a voice that says, What, who would I be without them, who would I be if I were completely naked, stripped to the buff, if I possessed absolutely nothing except myself: no clothes, no money, no country, not even a name, not love, not friends, nothing to eat, no place to sit, not a single book, not a note of music, none of those things that make life bearable and sometimes marvellous? That is the imponderable question, the moment of truth. What are we when all we have is life itself? Its limits instil a repulsive fear, but, at the same time, a secret yearning. Could I withstand it all, could I remain human? Or what if I gave in and sided with those who had already taken so much from me and who right now are after my very skin? How long would it take? The world is so terrible, so gorged, bursting at the seams with absurdities: violence and cruelty. I wonder what I would do in their place. What would I do if, as they had, I saw rise up before me those men of iron bent on annihilating me. Run. Run and keep on running. A lifetime of running in all directions to escape one danger after another, never knowing where to go, never knowing where they would strike. That is what they had done for centuries. Escape from some of them. Gain a few years. Watch the children grow. Then escape from others. Years and centuries passed. They were fed up, fed up and tired. Tired of having to fear. Tired of having to keep constant vigil. Tired of having to be distrustful. Tired of pulling up stakes at the whim of others' fury and lust for violence. And they told themselves finally: this time we are going to remain, we are not going to budge. No matter what happens, we are going to stay put.

It only had to be determined up to what point one continued to be human, up to what point it was worth it, after thousands of years, to cling to the idea that life is sacred, that man is sacred, made in God's image. The only way to be sure was to submit to the whims of chance, to allow oneself to be divested of all the effects accumulated day after day, generation after generation — money, honours, culture and even love — to find out what man really is, whether he is indeed reduced to a mere pouch of flesh, or rather a bag of bones. First, the instinct is to flee. But once that solution is exhausted, because there will always be other forms of hatred, *ad infinitum*, to torment you before you have even had time to unpack, then it becomes solely a matter of proving that you can resist anything, survive everything, that even the worst of conditions are bearable. Confront the worst and survive: and what if that is the only means of no longer being afraid?

A People of Memory...The little boy from the Warsaw ghetto, in the famous photograph, was not just a little boy. They all lived within him: the distant ancestor barely escaping the pyres of the Spanish Inquisition and slipping across the border into mediaeval France in the very midst of the Saint Bartholomew massacre, then taking flight to Germany and the Thirty Years' War and being pushed to the east, forever to the east, by hordes of scavengers and plaguers, catching his breath in Kiev before a pogrom propels him across the way, like a billiard ball, where German soldiers are in the process of walling up the ghetto.

The little boy from Warsaw had had enough of it. For centuries he had been walking his feet off. Okay, he says, the Spanish are fanatics. France will be more accommodating. He had seen so many hordes disembowel each other in so many languages...They're all the same...Enough of this being kicked around the world. All the same...It was his right to call an end to it, to stop, his right to cease running in all directions, his right to remain and to look him directly in the eye, to get close enough to see him clearly and to take the time to observe him: him, the Eternal and Sole and Multiple Enemy.

I had come to hate him, that little boy, with his hands raised above his cap in submission, him and all his kind — my kind — who had allowed man to reveal himself as he really is. In God's image. God as he really is.

And I was not the only one. Scarcely had some of those phantoms emerged from the horror when they were confronted with accusations: You didn't have to go along with it...you could have left in time.

But to where? Where could those six million bodies go all at once, bodies and voices and countenances, what country would have cracked open its door to allow them entry in time?

Okay. Well, then, you should have defended yourselves. And, inevitably, this refrain followed: You needn't have let them herd you to the slaughterhouse like so many sheep.

Never. Never was that said of the Armenians. Never were they reproached for their own deaths.

Finally, finally I understood them. Why they had taken their wives, their children, their grandmothers and marched where they were led. They knew. They knew that there would never be a real peace. Never. Never would there be a real life, neither for them nor for their children. Because, in this world, every accepted and tenacious difference provokes an equally accepted and tenacious hatred. It was thus that they went up in smoke. It was thus that they rose above the tips of the tall smokestacks.

It was at that precise moment that they came to Paris. In a way, it was they who saved me. She was an unusual woman, a strange combination of Katharine Hepburn and Golda Meir. And he, no, I cannot think of anyone with whom to compare him. In the final analysis, he was really quite unique. He had always thought so, and I believe he was right. Immense. Eyes of steel. An entrancing yet penetrating voice...A bona fide couple, those two. The impression one gets when in the presence of two people who have grown to resemble each other by dint of having always eaten the same things and having slept side by side.

One day, on their way back from New York or somewhere else, they stopped in to see us. He nearly lifted my mother off the floor when he embraced her, his diminutive cousin; and they all began to talk and talk, to exchange news concerning this person and that person, and to discuss life over there — talk uninterrupted by the concerned glances at our small kitchen, at the refugees' hodgepodge which refused to disappear after so many years...And Mama reddened, and all of us seemed to melt away in their presence because of our lack of courage and resolve and ideals, because we were confined here with our "next year in Jerusalem," still adrift in a foreign sea with the emptiness of next year in Jerusalem, where a dignified life awaited us. And we had no excuse whatsoever, unlike poor cousin Shmulik, who was truly locked in somewhere in Romania, truly unable to get out, he and his wife and kids and aging mother.

David stood up:

"And this child, your son? Have you even thought about him? That he must become a man? And you think he can do that here, perhaps?" King David's voice was scolding as he glanced around our lair, taking measure quickly, ever so quickly. He broke into a fit of terrible endless laughter, and for the very first time I saw my father bow his head.

It was only a few days before my *bar mitzvah*. I had memorized the entire *Parasha*, hundreds and hundreds of Bible verses to recite, and also a lengthy pronouncement in Yiddish, written by my father, who wanted me to show it off in full view of the assembly.

"...and you began to talk and talk and talk, and I fell asleep, as I do at the cinema when a film is boring, except that there, there were all those behatted people watching me. Finally, I got hold of myself, after a good quarter of an hour, but my poor dear, you went on and on and on before the assembly. And I, I had just returned from travelling all over America, holding meetings and presiding at banquets for months, and I think I dozed off again..."

I was laughing. She was teaching me, tenderly, to make fun of us, to laugh at myself.

The entire community had turned out to see me in my first big test in being a good Jew. My reward? Watches and wallets and transistor radios now stacked up and awaiting me in the office.

But David and Nadia, who have a knack and love for outdoing everyone else, hands down, had provided me with the most wonderful gift of all. They took me on board an ocean liner whose immaculate whiteness steamed proudly toward their large house in Tel Aviv. I was finally living out my dreams: in a Dickens novel, I was the young orphan who was ultimately discovered by his millionaire parents, I was Roddy McDowall between Katharine Hepburn and King David. In the evening, in the floating drawing room, I was fearful of betraying the imposture amidst the tranquillizing perfume of luxury.

I was a snob. At last.

So all Israelis do not resemble pioneers with faces drawn by nights of constant vigil and days of meagre pittance. Israelis could well be, like this couple, capable of waving a magic wand over a poor relative from the Diaspora.

She put things simply:

"We saw you up there, Daniel. And we told each other that that was no kind of life for a boy, that a boy needs to know something else!"

Something else...This something else was straight out of the movies, wasn't it? It couldn't be happening, in the banality of real life, it could only be a dream...

"No, no, not at all my child," she laughed. "You'll see. It exists. It's true. And listen: everything, absolutely everything is possible, you know, everything you want, if you want it enough."

Their place was so airy and serene...I forgot the gossips, I forgot the harsh ring of the telephone and its threats, I forgot our nook of a room and that God had granted himself ninety-nine percent of our space.

I even forgot God.

"You don't need a skullcap here. Here, the Israeli sky covers all heads."

They taught me to do away with the memories of my prison and my innumerable jailers. In the spacious living room opening onto a terrace scantily shaded by a young avocado tree, I learned a new rhythm of life: the seaside in the morning, reading in the afternoon and, in the evening, the lights of Dizengoff.

In a corner of their bookcase, I discovered, between Freud and Sartre, Nadia's prose works: her youth in Europe, the Galicia of her pogroms, the universities — Krakow, Berlin — and, finally, one day in the 1930s, the great departure, the kibbutz she founded in an arid land, she and her friends and brothers and sisters, when she was still quite young.

David and Nadia possessed the charm of dynamic, vital

people: they still believed in it, they could not stop believing in a virtuous state, the new frontier, eternally new...But they felt that I had fallen behind: a child of the Diaspora, another sensibility, indecisive, distrustful. And when my doubt led me to turn my eyes from theirs and to picture cannons and desert mirages, tanks and machine guns, that is when they defined for me, as gently and as cautiously as possible, their Israel-Auschwitz formula, as he had lived it.

And so I gave in to it and was immediately relieved of a heavy burden. I was happy to know that before long they would take a back seat to no one, happy also to know that they wanted to make a "Ben Adam" of me, a son of man, and, because *adamah* means earth, I would become a son of the Earth as well...

"This land, how I love this land."

The enchantment seized me on the road to Eilat, and she whispered in tones as low as an avowal of love:

"This land loves you, too, Daniel."

I flirted with them as adroitly as possible. For him, I related humorous anecdotes about our strange hodge-podge community. And he feasted on them, recalling faces from out of his past, in Sighet, his city...Each of the characters of my anecdotes brought back to mind another Jew he had known during his youth who had been lost in Sighet, his city...Those exile Jews, they are still as hilarious as ever! Despite his Zionist convictions, it reassured him to know that some of them existed elsewhere, that they were still the same: the same faults, the same sublimities, the same extravagances. Israel was not banking on them. Israel was banking on conformism, reason, modernity. As for Nadia, I needed only to talk about Paris, about the Latin Quarter, the Sorbonne, the only university she had missed out on.

For them, I learned Hebrew the way it is spoken in Israel. Within a few weeks I had become their little last-born. Their own children were all married and settled into a life that restricted their perspective to the distance between Tel Aviv and Jerusalem. But the three of us shared the same unalterably tragic view of the Genocide and, mysteriously, as much as they reassured me by guaranteeing me the permanence of the State of Israel, the refuge that would always be there for me, I comforted them by talking about a Europe that was on the mend and about communities like mine, which had come back to life.

It was here in Israel that they had planned a wonderful future for me:

"We have two sons, Daniel, but you are the one who is the most like me. We spend our lives trying to clear the hurdles. And I think that, like me, you can attain your every goal, even if those hurdles are unduly high through no fault of your own. They will have their share and you will have yours. You are our adopted son. But, in order for that to be, you must not disappoint us."

Touched and frightened, I set out to discover every aspect of this new frontier: reading, politics, swimming, tennis, the kibbutz.

My father sensed the conspiracy. The importance of my formal education escaped him. He would not agree to enroll me in a Tel Aviv *lycée* for the following term.

No matter. Besides, I was not completely sure I loved this country for anything other than the recreation it afforded me. No matter. The waning days of September. The beach that stretches from Tel Aviv to Jaffa. The heat from the Middle-East blast furnace was subsiding with the end of summer. Halos of blue-white radiance finished toasting me brown to near black. And I dozed off, bathed in the benevolence of renascent autumn.

Only a few days now. Take advantage. I am alone here. My arms and legs are alone, free, unshackled, and I stretch out like a young cat on its sun-drenched doorstep. Three months out of sight of the watchful eyes. I have flung my skullcap away, have sailed it over the tall cacti. And the never-ending impositions of my religion, morning, noon, night and the Shabbat? I have been liberated from them by King David himself. Not once, not one sole time, have I opened the pouch containing my two wretched *tefilin,* those small leather boxes with leather bands, filled with scriptural passages and worn on the left arm and forehead during weekday prayers. Just to touch it seemed to ruin the rest of the day...My arms and legs, my skin, my hair, even my eyes have changed colour. My entire body has become more supple, almost joyous, as though each cell had broken free and exulted in its new-found liberty.

Only a few days now. A few days of real family life: awaking to kisses, small bread rolls and a large bowl of cream, evenings on the terrace caressed by a loving breeze, the accompanying murmurs of friends and relatives...

Only a few days now, and back to the narrow, deserted stairway that resembles a vertiginous Soutine painting, back to the prison suspended in the void where our violet scenes will again resound into the depths of the dark and mute temple. Just a few days. Despite my efforts, I cannot help holding a grudge against those who had brought me here to learn about space and comforting solitude, intimacy and benevolence, who had given me all of that only to take it away again by sending me back to my father and confinement, back to the House of Sacred Forced Labour, where three sandpaper beings scrape away at each other until they howl.

Marseille. And then the sad, inverted *aliyah* to Paris. September 30th. The station, Gare de Lyon. A light, grey Paris drizzle. They are there, waiting for me. There they are, the two shrivelled parents, anxious to find out whether I have changed. Yes. I have grown taller. I have darkened in the sun. I am still calm and appeased by three months of open space, of free and sensual communion with the sea and the desert. A true "Ben Adam," a son of man. But not of this overbearing and suspicious man.

"Did you wear your *tefilin* over there?" he interrogated in Hebrew to put me to the test.

"Yes. Unfailingly."

My Hebrew is now more fluent than his.

"Every day?"

"Every day."

"And you're not even going to thank me?"

"For what?"

"Give them to me."

I hand over the small velvet pouch. From it he pulls a large one-hundred-franc bill wrapped in a handwritten note: "Thou shalt not lie."

"So there you are. If you had put them on once, just one time, mind you, you'd have found your pocket money..."

Paris. Nine months to endure before liberation.

But for the time being, I have been gathering strength in secret. And I keep telling myself: nine months to endure before feeling the warm sands...

While I am here I am going to do my best. Sacha is happy with me, and my teachers, too.

But the other. Never. He is always chiding me.

"Your actresses, your idols, your whores who stuff and pollute your mind, who invade your notebooks and clutter your walls. They do you no good whatsoever. Such idleness. Such frivolity. How shallow. How futile. Technicolor and tinsel, what taste!"

Let me be, what is the harm?
Let me be, alone
   to trace and trace again

such sweet endless folly
the magnificent broken arc of eyebrow
black velvet above purple iris
Let me be, alone to caress lustrous curls
and crimson lips
Let me dream dreams with other voices
dreams with curtains sheer not *parokhets*
let me have my sunlight goddesses
whose distant shimmering
light fills my room, fills my nights
For they struggle against the darkness
the howling corpses of my nightmares
It is not easy for me
it is not easy for them
Futility versus Tragedy
Alcove versus Dungeon Cell
Freshwater Spring versus the Flames
Chlorophyll versus the Odour of Smouldering Flesh

They have nothing to do with that,
you understand?
And that is why I absolutely need them
They were not, not in any way, involved in
that business
so they alone have the power to intercede
for me
so they alone have the power to combat
the horror

Let me be, alone not to confront
paralyzed with terror and nausea at the sight of
denuded skeletons of faces contorted by
hunger and suffering
Let me not hear the immense silent
cry
in the blackened depths of gaping mouths
gnawing the sulphurous air
Air, Air, Air...

Let me be, not to surprise the worm which already
   nibbles the glassy eye, bulging and misshapen
   in the deep cavity of a face
   which was a skull long before death

I have a perfect right to rest
   to have nothing further to do with that episode in
   smoke black and tibia white

I want, I must
   come back to royal blue to cherry red and
   to gold and to firm, soft flesh
Let me be with these bodies delicate and intact

Sing, lovely sorceresses! Speak! Bat
   your eyelashes
Do not above all bring me silence
Do not ring down the curtain before I
   fall asleep
If you do they will find me and
Bring me back for the final call
   naked and cold as ice in the courtyard where
   the hanged twist in the wind

I need to dream of an elsewhere
   where the streets are made of pasteboard
   of that far-off planet where no one is sought out:
   They did not have to wear
   the yellow star, Lauren Bacall,
   Tony Curtis — Benny Schwartz,
   Kirk Douglas — Danilovitch.
Impossible to pin up on my night-screen
   faces from here: Arletty, Simon, Guitry
   stars of that strange war

The Boulevard of Crime is not poetic realism
The Boulevard of Crime was everywhere here

How many departed knock-knock *shnel shnel*
    from rue des Rosiers?
How many children harvested on the grounds
    of the public schools of the French State?
How many people picked up, rounded up
    along the Grands Boulevards?
And how many visitors come to see
    at the Berlitz Centre, Boulevard des Italiens,
    the exhibit: "The Jew in France"?

My Sunset Boulevard has now faded into
    the Ocean
A street in Paris has come in its stead
    a long treeless street
    greyish half-light of buildings of sculpted stone
    arched entryways and concierges on the watch
That is when a reflection in the pale bakery
    window sets me to flight
I flee because they have discovered the garret
    where Edith and I have been hiding for
    two years

THEY took her away
She screamed in the stairway
Not my beautiful hair my long hair!
    my hair let it be!
Where you're taking me they'll take it from me
And from the paddy wagon she hollers up to flee to flee!
And I run and run
    past the solemn bourgeois houses on
    the Boulevard Montparnasse
At the Coupole it is coffee and
    croissant time
Ladies and Gentlemen of intelligent demeanour
    are watching, grieved, grieved for me, grieved that
    I must run like that

I hadn't even the time to tear off the star
But here is Orson Welles opening a manhole
He prods me with all the powerful mass of
    an old bison down the vertical stairwell
He must not have been able to stop them
    for their voices resound beneath the seeping
    archways
They track me through the tunnels
They find me

Before me the dead end and the wall on which
    my end is inscribed
Already a victims' lineup awaits me
Suddenly the wall breaches
Another glint of tunnel
I run and run breathlessly
A long inaudible cry paralyzes my body
I scream for help help
The passage is long to the open air
The distance between me and the uniforms narrows
My pyjamas are soaked and weigh me
    down
My pursuers are gaining
Shnel! Shnel! they howl
Shnel! Shnel!
The dogs' fangs rip into my pyjama tops
I cover my eyes *shnel! shnel!*

"...*Shnel! Shnel!* Daniel! It's half past seven! They'll be here in less than half an hour! Get dressed!"

I got out of bed and walked mindlessly to the door to let him in. He had already gone. Back in bed I am no more than an inert lump of downy flesh. Half an hour...A sharp breath of air filters in, through and around the rain-spattered window. Across the way, the office staff is filing in and pulling the canvas hoods from the typewriters. A strange place to work. Open today. Saturday. *Shabbat.* Three weeks ago, the youngest members of the congregation, those of my age, decided to create their own special services, a separate *minyan,* in the *Talmud Torah* hall adjoining my room, my hideout, my sanctuary.

I must escape before they arrive, I must get dressed and get out before they surround me...I must...I must have gone back to sleep. And now, how can I stir these flaccid limbs back to life in time to cross the long hall and run up the stairs to escape them? I must. I must at all costs. *Shnel! Shnel!* Their voices have already begun to echo up the stairway. But my bed has begun to rock with the soothing waves. The gentle breeze is closing my eyelids, its touch playfully caressing my eyelashes. The sun gently warms my loins. Golden curves of waist and hips...slip suddenly from desire's caress:

"*Shabbat shalom,* good morning!"

It is Philippe. They are already here, outside my door.

"*Ashrei yoshvei veitekha.*" Blessed are those who dwell in Your House.

Trapped like a rat. I have backed myself into my own corner, up against my own wall...And on the other side, prayers have already begun. They must not know that I am still here. I shall have to dig in, without a sound, and lie and wait. I glance up to see whether there is within reach a book in which I might take refuge. But I have already read everything.

For four long hours I shall have to listen to them, until the last one has left. Four long hours. I shall think about the long, flowing hair that blots out my nightmares. They cannot stop me...

"Hey, now, look at this! It's Daniel! You mean to say you're still in the sack?"

"And he's not alone, either. Look at that, would you. He's surrounded by all those lovelies!"

"Don't you want to come pray with your little friends, Daniel?"

They are all there, standing around my bed: fat Joseph, Gérard with his thick-rimmed glasses and Gabriel in that eternal blue blazer. They are all there, the ones who are constantly held up to me as models...

Damoel still in his pyjamas. Damoel surrounded by these young gentlemen in coat and tie. My limbs begin to thrash about. They do not understand. I tell them to get out. They do not realize. I throw back the sheets. And finally they leave, ashamed for having been so bold, for having seen. They close the door behind them without asking. And on the other side, services have begun.

"*Shnel! Shnel!* Daniel! Come out right now. Everyone is here."

Father is drumming on my door, reminding me of the special duties which await me beyond it.

I do not answer. He has left again. I reach out and grab for a shirt and feel about for my pants. *Merde!* It comes back to me all of a sudden. Last night I had undressed before coming down. The bed shakes with the pounding of my fists. *Merde!* Shit and double Shit! For once I had not taken the trouble and look what happens!

For four long hours they trumpeted into my eardrums. Four long hours. Before I could wash up. Before I could get dressed. Before I could piss.

"*Ashrei yoshvei veitekha*": Blessed are those who dwell in Your House.

The long hours spent at the *préfecture* in the vain attempt to become an official *Franzos* had finally discouraged my father.

But he soon gained a measure of revenge: he acquired an equivalent position and became one of the specialists empowered to certify the Jewish origins of applicants. Germany, endowed with a new prosperity by the United States, had decided at last to pay compensation for the six million smudges on its history. Many, it is true, refused the odious reparations: a wife or a newborn child gone up in smoke were beyond retail value...Others accepted, saying that they had been stripped of everything, including their gold teeth, and that Berlin was the richest city in the world.

For once, to be declared a Jew was necessary and without danger. In this case as in the other one, the selection process was of great importance, a process my father refined more and more day after day. Most of those who came to him and lined up to pass inspection as in the camps posed no particular problem, the ones with names like Cohen or Goldenberg, or with a number on their forearm, or whose Yiddish was still fluent and vigorous. Others knew they were Jewish, but no more than that: all their relatives had been rounded up and sent off to the camps. They were sole survivors deprived of family for so long, almost forever it seemed, and were incapable of relating anything at all about our customs because they had become totally, lamentably, assimilated. Some of them had the unlikely names of Picard, Schneider and Crémieux, and what was there to prove that they were not frauds of French or even German descent?

There was special treatment for such cases, a special interrogation conducted without obvious intent, during the course of which the applicant wound up revealing that there was somewhere within his depths a spark of *yidishkeyt*...My father adopted the principle that it was impossible, absolutely impossible, that everything, but everything, had been forgotten. He asked whether they had attended the *heder* to prepare for their *bar mitzvah*... Embarrassed, they had no knowledge of any of that. But the Hebrew alphabet? he would inquire.

"Where in the devil would I have learned it? In order to protect me, my parents had placed me in a Catholic school run by nuns!"

"And the synagogue? A place like this. Had you ever gone to one? Okay. Let's go back a little further. Couldn't you describe an expression or a gesture of, say, your grandmother? Let's see, can you tell me what she did on Fridays when she lit her candles? You can't say I'm not trying to help you out!"

Sometimes a small light shone out of a darkened past. "Wait a minute here. *Mémé*. Yes. She lit candles. That's right. And she covered her face with her hands...But what she said...I just can't recall what she said..."

Magnanimous, the secretary applied the inked stamp to the forms. It was not good enough for a Jew to be a Jew. He had to spend his life proving it or, indeed, according to the circumstances, disproving it...

There were those who were completely ignorant of Judaism. All they knew was that one day the police had come for their parents and they had never seen them again. They were defeatists, apathetic. My father showed them out and said,

"So sorry, Monsieur, so sorry, Madame...You are not integrated enough into our community life. Come back when you have proof, with witnesses, for example..."

He had adapted to his own use the bureaucratic techniques of the naturalization office: sorry, too assimilated.

"Proof? Witnesses? Do you really expect that, *mon petit* père?"

Thick-set with grey hair, an accent from the Paris *faubourg*, a heavy jaw, this Gabin look-alike had nothing in the least about him to inspire my father's confidence. He related his story: elderly parents who had become completely assimilated but who had had to wear the yellow star; they, too, had been sought out and taken away while he and his brother were acquiring the false papers that would allow them to pass into the free zone. After that, they had become *maquis*, had joined the Resistance. As for the parents, they had never returned.

"And that's not good enough for you, huh!"

The secretary insisted on the notions of religious instruction abandoned for centuries, it seemed, by this particular family. The secretary probed deeper and deeper.

"Okay. If proof is what you want, that's what you'll get. You'll see."

Six o'clock in the evening. The small office had begun to fill up. Worshippers had arrived for services. Madame Feldstein, who had been dozing in a corner for hours, stood up mechanically. The Jewish Gabin, with a slothful, almost majestic heaviness, faced my father and pulled his pants down slowly...Father blushed for the first time. Anything. Anything but that. Already, automatically, he was applying the inked stamp to the form.

"Monsieur, no, no! Monsieur! If you please! It really isn't necessary!"

"But if that's what it takes to convince you, I'm..."

"Now, Monsieur, let's be reasonable. I certainly wouldn't ask you to go so far..."

"But you were asking much more than that!" And he pulled out a colossal cock.

Apart from Madame Feldstein, who was looking on in fascinated horror, and my father, who was at the height of embarrassment, everyone seemed to be enjoying the scene.

"Mind you, that's the first time I've had to do that." He buttoned himself up and snatched the infamous certificate.

"Even under the Krauts, I managed to avoid that little formality. Fortunately, you see, I guess I just don't look like a Jew. And everybody left me alone, everybody but you. Well, good evening, gentlemen, and to you, Madame, please excuse me, but there was no other way. I had to do it. I had to..."

I was fifteen and she was twenty-five.

She had returned to us once again without the children. Her lifeless eyes sunken into their sockets looked like the eyes in my nightmares. My mother could not stop groaning and wringing her hands at the heart-rending sight of her. Father, I am no longer sure. I believe we saw less of him then. He always had instruction to give for an upcoming *bar mitzvah* or was busy distributing clothes to the poor. Edith lay silent for days on end, then sprang to life abruptly to shout out her misery. I also remember the near-serenity of certain days we spent painting portraits of each other, and days filled with the howling laughter of a miraculous truce when it was as if she was fifteen again and I was five.

The weeks went by. We even took her to a specialist at Sainte-Anne's. To no avail. Passover vacation was coming soon. Given her condition, someone had to accompany her, and I was chosen. It was a long trip and Edith was so fragile. We were to spend a night in London before continuing on by train to Liverpool, where I would remain for a few days. London: she had come to know only the train station after six years of being English. London: a train station like so many others, large and small, which merged in her memory — Kolosvar, Budapest, Vienna, Linz, Paris...London: the last stage of her migration to the west.

But the war was long ago, and it so happened that in those days, London, with its flashy zaniness, had a few youthful lessons to teach de Gaulle's Paris.

We found a rather inexpensive hotel, away from the centre of the city, near Euston Station. The thick carpets in the lounge, the mauve varnished furniture, the wallpaper's naive, childish design, the radio in each room, all that was far, so far from the drab hubbub surrounding my Paris cell. So far, so different, so removed in every sense...Here the subway was not our enemy; there was no memory of round-ups or of the last trainload. Here we could ask a bobby for directions without wondering whether he was old enough to have cleaned out the Marais quarter. London. Nothing to fear. No numbers on forearms. Here, no train from any station had ever left for Auschwitz.

So many things to see...We tarried in the National Gallery, Edith and I amidst the French Impressionists... And, riding in the upper deck of the red buses, we went from Piccadilly to Carnaby Street to Selfridges department store, in search of records, sweaters, the scripts of our favourite movies, between eating a bite at a Lyon's cafeteria and snacking on a hot dog — yes, a hot dog — because here there was no one to spy on us, nothing was prohibited. Edith was not very daring; she chose fish and chips. I teased her and prodded her:

"I'm sure that's cooked in pork fat! You'd better try a hot dog instead."

Edith did not dare. It was too late for her. For her, it was a mere matter of a few stolen hours, of small apertures between the two synagogues, the father's and the husband's, and what was the use of getting out of step for so little? She was old: twenty-five, two children.

But this immense, open, lively yet tranquil city brought something new to life within me: an insatiable hunger. I was finally learning to say yes to everything.

Between the Tel Aviv beaches and the long Paris hibernation, there were from time to time a few weeks with Edith, a few Yiddish weeks with Max the cantor and the two children who were already stammering out their prayers. I would go at *Rosh Hashanah*, and even *Yom Kippur* when it fell early in September.

They were "awfully British" weeks, too. The Kingdom knew full well how to naturalize everyone: houses all alike, a yard in front, a yard in the rear, an Austin parked nearby, a cup of tea at 11:00 A.M., and another at 5:00 and the telly, which, just before an old Hitchcock film, brought into every household the latest word on the Queen.

The days slipped away in this somewhat bohemian atmosphere which betrayed here and there Edith's continued ill-being. "Everything wasn't so all right" as Max claimed. The yard was a delirium of frenzied weeds, the flowers all seemed stillborn; a few lonely and meagre tufts of parsley survived amidst the jumble. The yards on either side, across the way and in the rear exhibited roses as large as cabbages and flamed with every colour of the fall spectrum. Edith took the children outside, and when discussions with the neighbour women turned to husbands, she began to talk about sex in such realistic terms that the mothers and their broods beat a very hasty retreat behind their bay windows, and pulled the starched velvet closed.

Their home had the necessary flowered carpets, the bedrooms were furnished with electric blankets, and in the drawing room the overstuffed furniture was arranged obediently in a semicircle around the telly. But in the dressers and wardrobes there reigned such a chaos that all the members of the household could do was shrug their shoulders. When guests were due, the cantor's wife gathered up the jumble and removed it from sight in a frenzy: chewing gum, nylons, banana peels, abandoned gadgets, and quick as a wink an adroit kick sent them into exile in the unexplored space behind the television set. The children shrieked with laughter. The guests arrived and then left again, and everything was forgotten where it lay.

No, Edith would never be British enough for her respectable neighbours, nor would she ever be Yiddish enough for the stern women of the congregation, just as she had never been Parisian enough for Paris. People said crazy and terrible things about her: they spoke of escapades and scandals, and this had caused Max to be removed from his position in Manchester. Here, she was not yet well known, but people were already talking about how between bouts of intense mysticism, during which she would chant and fast for days on end, she would sometimes disappear...Like that night she spent in the front yard of the young man for whom she had developed a passion and who, out of fear of compromise, had gone into hiding.

She laughed as she told me about it, and I laughed, too. I told myself that in a Richard Lester film with Rita Tushingham in the role of Edith and Albert Finney as fat Max, it would have been quite funny, very "knack," almost Carnaby...Carnaby Street, a baroque and shimmering world, the piercing shrillness of audio equipment, the violent strobe lights and the surrounding odour of incense. All that was beginning to be felt in Liverpool, too, especially on evenings when the little screen featured four gyrating long-hairs of whom the city was just starting to be proud. Even the youngest of the children, between two Hebrew lessons, bellowed "yeah, yeah, yeah" while scraping away at an imaginary guitar.

On Saturday evenings, those of my age crammed themselves into the humid, overheated night spots, amidst the noise of pounding drums. Most of the girls danced with each other, and when at last I won one over, we danced the jerk, then a slow dance, then a short walk across the soft, wet grass... I talked and talked and talked. My English was getting better. She laughed. And under the streetlight's yellow fluorescence, I finally got a good look at her: chubby face, acne, Clearasil. I was playing the game. I kissed her anyway. Fortunately, she almost turned away and said with authority, "No, not the French way, not with the tongue inside!" That meant spending endless minutes pressed up against that plastery lipstick. Then it was midnight, and she said, "Naughty Frenchy, bye-bye!" We exchanged addresses. "You'll write to me, promise? Don't forget!" I watched her walk away cold and damp in the Liverpool summer's night, her and the spatters of rain that clung to the roundness of her ass outlined beneath her skirt.

I returned to Edith and her obsessions. She guessed that I had been out flirting around. So I had to tell her exactly where I had been, "hot petting" or not. She smiled a forced smile, a combination of sisterly goodwill and bitter frustration...Summer was coming to an end. A humid breeze filtered heavily into the house, and with it Edith's face became even more lined. She berated me because I was outgrowing childhood. She abused Max more and more frequently, bellowing like a diva, while upstairs, in the bedroom with the Mickey Mouse wallpaper, the children moved about in a hush.

On the London-Paris nonstop, at the outer reaches of the Gare du Nord, I learned that the last car of the train, my train, had been reserved by Elizabeth Taylor, the queen of my thousand and one sleepless nights...Liz and Burton, *the* scandal bearers. So on the car-ferry, instead of staring over the side into the sea-green depths, I could have gone to the bar and drowned myself in the violet fathoms of her irises.

Wait until everyone else had left the train. That is surely what they would do. There were very few people there to witness Cleopatra's arrival in Lutetia, only a handful of onlookers — just as there had been long ago in Rome — to gawk in hostile silence at the overly rich and overly beautiful couple. When they stepped down to my level, I picked up my travel bag. And then I was walking almost at their side. She, in rather sober attire that day, did not look at all like the witless Californian she often chose to portray. She was infinitely more dignified, infinitely more beautiful than on the screen. Beyond certain limits, no doubt, the camera cannot capture magnificence and must therefore be used to deify visages of a more regular and banal sort. There was something in her fixed stare, a coldness which no filmmaker had been able to exploit, the distant coldness of a sphinx.

A few moments later, she disappeared into a taxi. And I went back to my room where she became again what she had been before, a page out of a magazine, made to brighten the austere walls of my cell.

Back in Paris, my only escape was to slip into the intimate confidence of families that seemed to be governed by harmony and plenitude. Without thinking about it, I always chose people to whom he could not object, those who were more sure of themselves, who were better educated and sometimes even more religious than he.

How could he object to the prolonged evenings at Sacha's where I helped his daughter Ingrid finish a Hebrew translation? In exchange for which, of course, I accepted holiday meals and Sunday automobile rides in the forest. That was my vice in those days, belonging to a family other than my own.

All the same, I had to do it in moderation, for I observed my father's jealousy beginning to mount, his envy of those well-to-do bourgeois and practising Jews against whom he found nothing to say. And my mother succeeded in troubling my mind with a simple little phrase:

"Are you quite sure they're not going to grow tired of you in the long run? People don't like outsiders in their home."

All the more so since one evening, Sacha, having tired of all the young people who swarmed about Ingrid, suddenly resumed his role as head of the household and showed us all the door.

With his long strides, he caught up to me while I was waiting for the bus.

"Please don't be offended, Daniel, I got carried away. I hope you're not upset with me."

And since the bus was late in arriving, he took my arm, led me to his car and drove me home. Upset with him? Never would my father have chased after me to apologize for anything.

Ingrid was in my class. So was Marianne Keller. With Marianne something wonderful happened: that beautiful rare friendship between a boy and a girl. Well, we had attained the impossible. No ridiculous games of sleight-of-hand; that would be for someone else. No intimate gropings: that would be for later. All we wanted was to prolong our childhood.

Marianne and I used to cut classes and steal away to the coziness of her well-appointed apartment.

"You're certainly home early today," Madame Keller would say softly and without the slightest suspicion. Madam Keller: as slim and lovely as Anouk Aimée, little did she know that she was saving us from Friedman.

Often, in the evening, she would ask me to stay for supper. She lit candles, and then there was asparagus, followed by a finely roasted chicken and strawberry tarts.

Marianne's father, a former antique dealer with a passion for the fine arts, had seen his business fail. He had nevertheless managed to recoup somewhat sadly, yet valiantly by getting into the lingerie trade. From the disaster, he had been able to salvage a small varnished painting in gay colours depicting a group of cherubic nymphs frolicking in a meadow full of flowers.

"My dear Daniel, to you, an art lover, I am going to confide something: Rubens and Brueghel, not the Elder but the Brueghel the Younger, the exquisite Brueghel de Velours, sometimes worked together. It is quite possible that these lovely creatures were painted by Rubens and that the jungle of spring flowers was done by the other."

When I stayed overnight, Madame Keller, who had no son, folded out the daybed in the living room. For a few hours, everything became as relaxed and comforting as before, when I had been in Israel with David and Nadia.

At the approach of my sixteenth birthday, my father began to talk about naturalization again.

"They will offer you the option, and you'll accept. Then, since we'll have a real French citizen in our family, Mama and I will follow suit."

Of course nothing would change at home; but at least there would be no more lines, no more interminable waiting for the most insignificant document, for any little trip we might care to take.

All that was fine, except that I no longer wanted to play the game. Before, when I was a child, in that strange other world imported into our home from the Carpathian Mountains of northwestern Romania, when I was a child and they tried to pull me back into a world that no longer existed, when I was a child, I had revered as long as possible the country in which I had really been born. But later, when they had finally succeeded in imparting to me the fear of others, I had grown accustomed to the barrier that separated me from the country in which I lived: it became a feeling of freedom for me, of being from everywhere and nowhere at the same time. The Wandering Jew? Why not?

In those days, youths around the world dreamed of finding refuge "anywhere out in this world"...We wanted to be *apatrides* from everywhere, at home everywhere, home sweet home in Nowheresville. I revised my school comps beneath the boughs in the Vert-Galant, that pleasant little spot on the Ile de la Cité which attracted young people from everywhere. Soon I would close my exercise book and stretch out on the grass to listen to the latest generation of beatniks describing the ground they had covered, barefoot, with guitars slung across their backs. I learned Bob Dylan's songs, discovered Kerouac and dreamed of a voluntary, juvenile vagabondage. Tomorrow those Americans would turn around and head East...The march of the anti-pioneers would turn on itself and head back: "Go East, young man, to the Orient!" would soon be the cry. And so now my *apatride* parents, having grown old and tired, wanted to talk about naturalization, normalization and, if they weren't careful, maybe even assimilation.

"Try to understand, Daniel. Papers! Papers! A man isn't anything without papers! A man has to be officially recognized."

"Sure. It was that need to be recognized that led them straight to Auschwitz! That made the Nazis' work all the easier. They all lined up, very polite and well-dressed, to be checked off by the authorities. They did all that just to be official!"

"But, but, but...Come now, let's not dramatize. Those days are gone forever. Get them out of your mind. That's all in the past."

And he had the nerve to tell me that!

"But, Daniel, what bothers you so much about taking this step?"

What bothered me...It was hard to say, exactly. I was becoming pessimistic, more pessimistic than he...French? Why French? Because I was born here? Because I happened to speak this language owing to a misadventure in our long march toward an aborted *aliyah*? No. Certainly not. I liked the idea of being from nowhere, the idea of being nothing; and if another madman should rise in his place, it might be the only means of making my enemies forget my very existence.

"And that way you'll be able to do your stint with the Army, and everything will be in order with the military."

The poor man! Unwittingly, he had just put his finger on a real source of panic. Eighteen months of pimply, one-hundred-percent-male cohabitation in barracks, usually in Germany. Communalism had long been a monkey on my back. But the other, the Army, somewhere near Frankfurt, concentrated like that, in a camp...

"And who knows," he continued enthusiastically, "agreements with Israel are in the works. You might be able to do your tour of duty there!"

It was getting better and better...Surrounded by Sabras, native-born Israelis, over a hundred degrees in the shade, somewhere along the Syrian border, bullets to dodge from the Golan Heights. There would be girls, it is true, but Israeli girls. Impossible to know how to deal with them. Flirt with them and find yourself twisted around in a judo hold, fail to do so and gain the reputation of being a *pédé*, a fag.

"This miraculous agreement will bestow on me the right, if France goes to war — and when that happens it goes on and on — or else if Israel does — it's shorter there but, frankly a chronic event — the right to commit myself to two fronts. Don't you have anything better to propose?"

The war in Algeria. The war in Algeria had just ended. Whatever happened to the soldier we met in the small square? And in my mind's eye I saw again those Vert-Galant wayfarers, bearded and blue-eyed, who talked about Hiroshima...I understood why they dressed the way they did, in the exact opposite of "naval" attire. No doubt they were fleeing a war they would otherwise have to fight soon, far from home, even though their country was in no danger.

No. Certainly not. That did not fit in either. Being a little Jew from the Diaspora suited me just fine for the present.

"And then those few months of roughing it..."

"...will make a man of you, my son," I declaimed with angry irony.

"Daniel, Daniel, please, don't make fun. It's for us, you understand, we're too old now to start over in Israel. And I, I want to be official, to belong..."

One fine June day, I went down to the *commissariat* to

get stamped. It was called "*Français par option,*" citizen by choice. It made everyone happy. I finally succeeded in giving them a small measure of *nakhes.*

And in two years I could look forward to the joys of being drafted.

The time had come when the city lights finally began to penetrate the heavy foliage of the chestnut trees and the mysticism that Sacha spread throughout the school grounds. Teddy and I shared a common passion: the cinema. Or, more precisely, pictures, moving and otherwise. The Boulogne Studios lay only a short distance from the *lycée*. Teddy went there with his Nikon strapped to his shoulder, ready to snap a photo that he would sell to a trade magazine or a prominent newspaper. Perhaps one day there would be the miraculous click and his photo would be seen around the world and his career would be launched.

I went there for an entirely different reason. I did not photograph anyone. I did not ask for autographs. I went there solely to assure myself that the faces which had struggled so courageously against my phantoms were not mere celluloid illusions, that my dreams were at least as real as my nightmares. We haunted the neighbouring cafés, slipped into the corridors leading to the sets, a false garden or a pasteboard street, from which we were chased as soon as the trial takes were finished, as soon as the doubles filed out to give way to the stars. No matter. We had seen them.

My sorceresses. Fragile and delicate. Protective of their faces. They appeared for the briefest of instants, tense from the ritual that precedes the shooting of a new sequence. Teddy focused his camera and then saw nothing.

"Who was she?" he inquired too late, as Sophia Loren swished out of sight, as tall and erect as a statue of Minerva.

I was not listening. I had become my own double as in a special effect. Another me followed in their wake, like Gary Cooper, who had been able to defy the laws of gravity in *Peter Ibbetson*.

Teddy, Jean-François, Marianne, Claude, Elsa and I. To all appearances we were high schoolers like all the rest. We lent each other books, talked about the latest Losey film, met at the corner café to discuss what really had to be done and seen during the coming week and to pool our funds. Impossible now to restrain myself, even on Saturday afternoons. We had to make up for lost time, to discover all the masterpieces that predated us and were being rerun on rue Champollion: *Citizen Kane, la Règle du jeu, African Queen*...At the Bobino, we waited for intermission to sneak in by way of the artists' entrance. How deliciously deceitful! And we committed the crime again, to be able to hear Barbara sing us her wonderful declarations of love.

We thus persuaded ourselves more and more each day that we were indeed like everyone else, because we all liked the same films and the same books, because we danced to the same tunes as the other members of our generation.

Where was the difference, then? One minor detail: Teddy, Jean-François, Marianne, Claude, Elsa and I were all Jewish, and that gave us a special feeling of security as we walked down the boulevard Saint-Michel — exactly like the young *yeshivah* students centuries before who locked arms when they crossed a wide boulevard in Kiev or Krakow...

The summer sent me back to David and Nadia. As the years passed, they sensed — even before I did — that something was binding me more and more to Paris, Paris which after a few weeks began to give me pangs of homesickness. I had to see a French film. Had to. Had to seek out from among the crowd of Dizengoff strollers someone with whom I would not have to speak that beautiful, overly simple, overly limpid biblical language. David was quite aware of it, and Nadia was ever so close to admitting it and understanding it: for years on end they had been receiving this promising young man into their home, in the country which guaranteed his very survival, and now he seemed to be claiming his right to the Diaspora! David became indignant to the point of being sadistic:

"But you haven't seen anything, my poor boy...I was at Auschwitz! I was there! Do you really believe that after all that's happened you can look forward to making a life for yourself over there, on that fucking continent? You're a Jew. And everyone knows it there. All your delusions won't be worth a thing. You'll think and reason and suffer like a Jew."

"I can't give you a satisfactory answer. Hebrew is awkward for me, it makes my arguments seem simplistic, and you take advantage of the situation to try to make me look stupid."

"Because you think you know French! Listen, I don't speak French, but I know that you don't actually feel a single word of it. Do you understand what I mean by feel? You are made of different stuff, of another turn of mind. French will always be a sterile tool for you. You think you understand Montaigne, Balzac or Sartre? You will never have real access to them. Look at yourself closely, inside and out. You look like all your little Diaspora friends: crusty, fearful, pretentious, no ideals, with no possibility of a future...You're like your parents: deceptive, weak-willed, primitive!"

"Now, David, stop hassling the poor boy," Nadia ventured once everything had been said.

I ran down the stairs to flee from them as I had fled from my parents only a short while before. I took the first bus to Jerusalem, in hopes of finding a little peace...

Jerusalem. King George Street. Tall cypresses. A beautiful green border rising high into the air. On the other side of Jaffa Street, the way climbs toward the old city. The past envelops me suddenly. I am surrounded by the whining strains of a small violin played by an old musician from a Russian village... Meah Shearim: a displaced piece of Europe, an impossible ghetto oblivious to our pogroms. Here, for generations, the dilapidated houses have been passed on from father to son. Here is where Israeli propaganda stops: "Houses are popping up like mushrooms; Israel is being built in a day." No. Not here. Here, Israel is content to go on modestly and peacefully behind the tall cypresses, beyond the sounds of bulldozers and machine guns, without the progressive silhouettes of giant cranes to infringe upon the tender blue of sky. On the other side of the trees, girls, furtive and stiff, are going their way undaunted by the heat; they are wearing flowered taffeta dresses —

mauve, yellow or turquoise — whose long sleeves are carefully buttoned at the forearm. Their skin is nearly a ceramic blue. Across the way, on the other side of the street, in the modern city, there is a parade of tall, muscular and copper-skinned Amazons dressed in shorts and khaki shirts. Quickly, ever so quickly, the smaller ghetto girls are running their errands without looking at anyone or anything, their moist eyes panicked above pale, freckled cheeks and framed with braids of red hair. Do they even know Hebrew? Later, in any event, they will speak Yiddish with their mothers. The sacred language is for men. And only for studying the sacred texts.

In Meah Shearim, people do not progress. People study. The One Hundred Gates were fabricated to lock time in. A closed circle with no connection to the supermen of the new city. They live sparingly, with only one thing in mind: their immense love for God and for their fellow man. For their country? For Israel? Less so. It so happens that some of the most religious ones even feel close to the Arabs; they do not recognize the State of Israel because Israel cannot be reborn until the coming of the Messiah. And how will they be able to recognize the Messiah? Will the Messiah merely take the form of a human? And what if it were a state of grace, a moment in Jewish history when all Jews were good, studious, peaceful and free from all threats of persecution? Is such a golden age even possible? That is what has been discussed for generations in all the city's small *batei midrash* and *yeshivot*. The words rise into the summer's heat punctuated with question marks and suspension points, up and up, above the ill-kept yard behind the tall cypresses, soaring far and farther still, toward other communities, toward brothers in Brooklyn and Moscow and those on the rue des Rosiers.

The houses are as dusty as the yards: awkwardly built, no planning, no architecture. Need another room? Build it on the roof. Weeds nearly as tall as trees abound in luxuriant freedom and point their thick, uncomely leaves skyward between dripping clotheslines.

Old men dressed for winter move along lethargically with their sons or students always at their side, young people already as heavy as the great flightless birds of the earth. Behind thick lenses and circled by heavy rims, their eyes are locked in a blind stare.

The tourist can look directly at them, or even mock them, and it will not bother them in the least. The tourist can appear to be very knowledgeable, to be well travelled, but they have better things to do. They must race against cascading time. They know that no one knows anything; for no one, up to the present day and time, has been able to peel away the cortex, to analyze anatomically, to sound the depths, to assimilate and classify all the signs of the inexhaustible Torah. Thousands of years remain to be deciphered. So many mysteries hidden in the past. How can anyone even think about the future? How can anyone live in the present?

From backyards come the cries of children and mothers who scold them while doing their mending on the rear balcony. Their wigs — yellow, brown or red — make the women's tranquil faces appear even paler.

The streets smell of slightly rancid walnuts. In the many schools, pupils, crowded together and seemingly unaware of the stifling heat, sway to and fro as they chant and implore.

Perhaps my parents...Perhaps here, for all of us, things would have been different, possible...

The baccalaureat exams that year were the most difficult in recent memory. Claude, Teddy and I managed to survive the written portions; we decided to study together for the orals.

I told myself that my father would leap for joy, that this would be even better than the day not long ago when I was declared "fit for military service."

"You passed. That's nice, my son, that's fine," he said absent-mindedly, without taking his eyes from the receipts he was typing. "But don't forget that the main thing is to be a good Jew."

This time, it seemed, I had become too naturalized...No one even mentioned it at the evening meal. It smelled of something less desirable, the university, of goys and shiksas...

There was a three-week vacation with Edith in Liverpool; I was able to steal away for days at a time to discover a misty

Scotland and the shores of her large lakes, to hitchhike alongside fun-loving Saxons and lovely backpacking girls.

Only an hour till train time. Edith must have sensed my joy that morning. I could not pretend any longer. I could not even say the words she expected: "I don't like goodbyes." I had become self-centred, an egotist, and I was happy to be one and not to feel the least bit guilty about it.

I forgot to say thank you for everything, there is nothing like family, I hope we'll see each other again soon. I was playing with her little son instead of embracing her closely, instead of acting out the well-rehearsed theatrics of my usual departure, instead of swearing that nothing in the world could ever weaken the bonds between us. Only an hour till train time. Did I provoke her by dreaming aloud about the new friends I would be making, about the small Paris bistros, about the music and the books, about everything she had taught me to savour and of which she had subsequently been deprived? What sparked the terrible scene that was to follow? Something completely inconsequential, no doubt. I must have asked too light-heartedly to see the train schedule or for help in closing my suitcases.

"So you're finally going to desert, are you, after all we've done for you?"

"But, Edith, it's the logical thing to do. I have to make my own way; it would be stupid to let everything go down the drain now. Aren't you the one who used to tell me that I'd have to learn to be a man, to stand on my own two feet?"

"A man, yes...But a Jew before all else! The more I see of you, the less I see you are a Jew. You're no longer one of us, of our people. OUR PEOPLE! OUR PEOPLE! Do you want me to tell you what you are? You're a TRAITOR!"

Her speech began to falter, her words ran together hoarsely in long screeches. She frightened me, but I could not let on for anything in the world. I had to stand firm, I had to resist. It was vital, and the best thing to do was to say nothing at all.

"You have nothing to say. You know I'm right! You're worthless, a failure! Who do you think you are? You play at being a hippie. You go out with girls. What futility! How shallow! But you've always been shallow. No sense of responsibility. You're the last male in the family, you know. The others are all dead. Assassinated at Auschwitz! The last one. Have you ever thought about what that means?"

Only a quarter of an hour and the bus will be taking me to the station. I am still holding back, containing myself.

"I did what I could, what I had to do, what was expected of me. I married a pious Jew, I gave our parents two grandchildren raised in the strictest tradition...But it's up to you to perpetuate our name, and all you can think about is your own little world. And all the while our parents are growing older...You're an egotist, an egotist and a parasite, a PA-RA-SITE, you understand?"

I do not understand anything. I have already made my way up to the Mickey Mouse bedroom where I am comforting my nephew, who took to his bed because his mother was screaming. And here is Debbie home from school, a tall, nine-year-old gazelle. There is just enough time to squeeze her in my arms; she covers me with fresh, moist kisses. Like an apple brought in from the cold.

Downstairs, Edith pulls herself together as best she can and says, "I'll go to the station with you. I don't want us to leave each other like this."

A little later, on the platform, she whispers:

"Don't be too upset with me. I was hard on you only because it was time for you to leave. I should have waited for a better time."

Hard? She did not say "unjust," only "hard." She may have been a little overbearing, but she still believed that what she had said was true. I force a smile because my train is being announced. I lean out the door as the train pulls away. I do not wave goodbye. I cannot, do not want to do anything but maintain a straight and expressionless face until her silhouette has disappeared into the yellowish fog.

In London, between trains, I saw Liz and Burton scream at each other in *Who's Afraid of Virginia Woolf?*. I was somewhat reassured as the train rumbled on toward Paris, and blessed Hollywood for proving that that sort

of thing happened, that it was even somewhat fashion-
able for people in the suburbs to hate each other.

Seated in a circle on the carpet in Teddy's large living room, we listened to the tender vibrato flowing from the record player. Joan Baez's voice lent a strange Gaelic air to the nostalgic *"Pauvre Rutebeuf "*:

> *Que sont mes amis devenus*
> *Que j'avais de si prés tenus*
> *Et tant aimés...*

They were all there. Marianne was humming quietly, her long, fine hair falling gently onto her shoulders, her large, dark, puppy-dog eyes reflecting the candle Teddy had placed on the varnished table. Soon, from out of his room at the end of the hall, he brought his inseparable Nikon: the music was about to be accompanied by the familiar clicks of that ever-present contraption. Elsa was there, too, feeling somewhat tense and out of place and forever looking around for something to touch. And there were Teddy's friends from outside of school: Robby, the pick-up artist, and Karol, who had recently arrived from Poland and dreamed of becoming a filmmaker like Polanski. Maurice, as he had the habit of doing in math class, swept back a patch of rebellious hair in a deft movement. Michel was there also, in a corner, his long skin-and-bone silhouette scarcely visible against the folds of the red velvet drapes. I sat there in the midst of them, with Isabelle's heavy head in my lap and her soft, plump and dimpled arms loosely and vulnerably around my waist. She still loved me, and I still did not love her.

Soon we would be at the University, and little by little we would grow apart, pass or fail, go our separate ways. Our collective mother, the Jewish community, was pulling strings, dealing the cards, controlling the outcome. The community spoke to us through our parents. Already they were determining our professions, selecting our future friends, choosing our future spouses, deciding in which country we should live.

(One more click, Teddy. Take it and don't mess it up. This is our group photo.)

Ah yes, Teddy, soon to be *the* Edouard Wexler, the "new Cartier-Bresson" as you called yourself laughingly.

Gare Saint-Lazare. Destination Folly.

I had taken many trains. They had carried me to a torpid Negev and a misty Liverpool. Henceforth those landscapes were no longer a part of me...Modern literature. Modern, modern! No more anachronisms, archaisms, no more scribblings bound in worm-eaten leather.

Modern. The new Nanterre campus. The heck with the Sorbonne and its marble, its frescoes and its statues... Oh! here's my baccalaureat certificate! But where in the world is my identification card? Just in case...You can never be sure...

My mother is ironing the shirt purchased yesterday on the boulevard Saint-Michel (small collar, ochre stripes). I was even allowed to buy a new pair of pants, and for the beginning of this school year I decided not to trim my hair.

They are observing someone they do not know, someone they have never really looked at, someone they have only looked after.

Gare Saint-Lazare. Destination Folly.

Salle des Pas Perdus. Platform number two. Now the wheels are sliding over the wet rails. Rain is falling on the Asnières cemetery. I peer out at this ordinary suburb drowned in grey. Already the fogged-up windows are transforming the coach into a classroom. Students are filling its space, and cigarette smoke mixes with the wet-dog odour coming from hair and clothes. I was worried about missing the station, but now all I need to do is follow the crowd.

I look at our images reflected in the window. I note with pleasure that I seem commonplace. If they only knew how happy it made me to look normal, to be purged of all strangeness, of all the peculiarities that have plagued me from birth! They would surely be astonished, these young Parisians who dream of, live on and feed off other people's folklore: couscous, bossa nova, Mao's *Little Red Book*, feijoada, sangria, tequila, balalaikas and all the rest.

Normal. Commonplace. I love the commonplace ugliness of the greyness into which we are now penetrating. I inhale the sweet and wet air, I march happily and willingly into this paragon of ugliness, the barracks-like buildings, the doors already smeared with the graffiti which are for me the symbols of freedom.

First-year students' registration. Building A. End of the hall.

I hear my footsteps echo up from the university

grounds. It is only the everyday noise of feet upon flagstone. But my senses perceive it otherwise, for me that noise has become the imaginary sound of gallant boots against the ancient paving stones of a Sicilian castle, as in Visconti's *The Leopard*, when, before the ball, the count penetrates the Pantaleone courtyard.

Here it is. Office number six. Many of my future classmates are already waiting: Combey, Drut, Garnier...There are so many that I have the time to think about those wrath-filled days again, the three of us cooped up there, shut in, incarcerated, one would have thought, for life.

So I have not yielded, what I so feared has not come to pass. I know what they are going to say: you will try to forget that you are one of us, you will betray us all, you have already betrayed us! As though it were possible to forget. I am so tired. I am only bent on recuperating, recuperating and living. I just want to be here, to fit in, to be one among many, one among the others.

My student ID is in my pocket. What a wonderful feeling, the result of all that energy expended over the years, from the days of the wasps in the vegetable garden and the bees buzzing in the burning air, just to be able to hear my footsteps on these flagstones of freedom, which — though no one knows it yet — are soon to become the flagstones of mutiny.

They always told me that even if I wanted to forget, there would always be someone to remind me, however innocently.

Maybe so. But who is talking about forgetting?

No matter. They were right. They will always be right. I can try to escape from them, but I shall never be able to escape from the others. From the very first days there were questions from well-meaning acquaintances, questions and voracious curiosity.

And then there was you, my love. Inadvertently at first, then with so much benevolent insistence, you made me stand up to them, to confront them and myself. And you did not want me to be commonplace either, you did not want me to be like all the others...

In the beginning, I saw only your profile beneath the high, flat ceilings of the Nanterre amphitheatres where classes were held. Always in profile. Rarely did you direct your gaze toward the rostrum. You usually appeared distracted, and I wondered where your mind wandered. You were seated so far from me in those enormous amphitheatres, but I had learned to zoom in on you, as though through a telephoto lens, to focus on the hollow of your cheeks, to observe the slow deterioration of the Bic pen on which you chewed constantly.

After class, I tried to approach you in the mass of students who were trying to find out where their next course was located. But you had already slipped away and were at the end of a long corridor strewn with leaflets. You moved through them as though you were scuffling through a carpet of autumn leaves. One last glimpse of a fold of your narrow coat and the translucent glass door closed behind you. Where were you headed? Who was waiting for you so impatiently?

Weeks passed. I tried, tried to get you to while away some time in the cafeteria, but you always had something to do elsewhere. No matter. I was gaining ground. I already knew every facet of your face, from every angle, and my hands could form its every contour. I had even heard a name, Pascale. As for the mysterious world of your mind, not a clue.

Today I finally got up the courage to ask you where you were always running to in such a hurry. You were rather vague, but I did learn that it had to do with artists, the performing arts and photographers. I was inquisitive, perhaps I appeared too interested...(Pictures, images, everywhere I turn, a world that will not let go.) Then you seemed to stiffen:

"As many of them as there are, they all bore me, even bother me. I have the feeling that they are eating away at me, that every click of the camera, every photograph is robbing me of something important, something inside me which is mine alone. Do you know what I mean? They are eating away at my soul. I don't know what it's worth, really, but it seems to me that no one has the right to do that to anyone."

And then you were gone, more quickly than usual. No doubt out of the fear that you had seemed too self-centred or even odd.

And there I was again, alone in the shadows of the

broad corridor. A mere ten metres away, Godard was shooting his film *La Chinoise*, and for once I did not even care. For me, the spotlights had grown dim; all I could do was dream about what I really wanted to tell you...

A mere ten metres away, Godard was shooting *La Chinoise*, but I, yes, that's it, I was thinking about my Hassidic ancestors who refused to be photographed because the human image belongs to God alone...I was thinking about the rushing figures — like you — in Meah Shearim, those who stop only to curse the image-seekers while covering their faces. Next time, I swore it, next time I would tell you, Pascale, that, strangely enough, you were like my ancestors...No. I would not say that, but how could I make you know that I had understood? How could I make you understand, without seeming to be an idiot, that I wanted to know you, wanted to know your very soul?

They are always right, the parents. It is impossible to live in a state of unawareness, of oblivion. Hordes of class-mates, Gentiles or worse — assimilated Jews "seeking their identity lost generations ago" — crowd around me. They have caught the scent of folklore. My anonymity has not held up for very long. I have had to resume my role as a Jew, more Jewish than the others, the Jew among Jews. Whether at the university during the day or at home at night, that is how they want me. In the halls and in the amphitheatres, I explain what my father has taught me...But you, Pascale, you are not one of them. Those are the very moments you choose to slip away, to vanish.

How strangely things came about. You did not say anything for a very long time. You waited for me to stop talking, to tire of wearing this new skullcap. Then, little by little, you began to ask questions, to probe, but never too deeply, never down to the nerve, to the threshold of my misery.

Gare Saint-Lazare. Destination Folly. A narrow and muddy boarding area with no barrier was all there was for passengers going to and coming from the university. We had to walk along the avenue de la République, an endless corridor of ankle-deep mud bordered by giant cranes and Arab workers who were forever opening, closing and reopening the foundations of buildings soon to constitute our new campus.

While awaiting this glorious future, every morning at ten minutes to eight, the long stream of students rushed along in the rain (and how it could rain then) to crowd up against the hot drink machines, which were always out of order.

The exiled students of Nanterre la Neuve were frustrated here and complained bitterly about having narrowly missed being accepted at the Sorbonne. Here there were no traditions, no cafés; it was impossible to take one's studies seriously in this construction site where nothing ever happened.

A few students organized meetings, visited the nearby slum areas and opened a dialogue with the immigrant workers. Little by little attitudes began to change and spirits began to rise.

Several groups had formed. There were about a dozen of us; we shared class notes and saved each other places in the cafeteria.

I was watching you, Daniel. You intrigued me. All the trouble you went to, to create some sort of atmosphere, to stimulate conversation, to make contacts...

One would have thought you were fresh out of prison.

Just as soon as you left, even for a few minutes, the mood changed, the group seemed to disintegrate, to unravel. I did not talk much, I loved the flood of words, the cigarette smoke entranced me, as did the comfort of our designated spot near the bay window where we watched the rain fall, the October rain, the December rain, the February rain.

Though I did not say much, I already felt that you were destined to become a permanent part of my life. I needed you. I needed those green eyes that hardly ever blinked, needed to feel your gaze upon me — long, slow, insistent but not at all bothersome. What touched me was their wariness, their circumspection, which betrayed the joyous and abundant energy of your words. Your gaze made me feel that we had known each other forever, and it was painful even to think that some day you might walk out of my life.

"**Y**ou live with your parents too, do you?"

The percolator gargled. Next to us a worker attacked a pinball machine. The jukebox vibrated with a Ferré song: "*C'est extra.*"

You do not hear that I have answered yes. The Gare Saint-Lazare is regurgitating its flood of people, and almost all of them, it seems, are headed straight for our little coffee shop. The smell of brewing coffee surrounds us; you lean closer to be able to hear what the others are saying. Elise, Laurence, Marc, all of them caught up in the general flow of things, tuned mechanically to student concerns. Their soft voices weave through the background noise. Their words reach us in nonsensical snatches: university, profs, general studies, leaflets.

"How's that?"

"A synagogue."

"Are there religious pictures everywhere or what?"

(Your laughter is a draught of spring water amidst the torrent of metallic sounds. I love your cinemascopic smile and your eyes, which, joyfully, react in an instant, even before the laughter escapes from your lips.)

"No, I meant it. I live in a synagogue. I do. I'm not kidding. I swear it."

"Since when?"

"I don't know. For a long time. Almost forever, I guess."

"He has taken me there," Marc interjects sententiously. "It's fabulous! You can talk with God every day..."

Your teeth are clenched. How did you guess that he didn't understand? My eyes thank you. Yours, intense and darkened now, ask me why.

"My father works in a synagogue. His office is downstairs and we live upstairs."

"A live-in arrangement?"

"Yes, something like that, I suppose."

"Your Father, is he a sort of Jewish priest, I mean, uh...a rabbi?"

"Sort of...If you like. But not exactly. He does a bit of everything...Religious instruction for the children, *bar mitzvahs*, weddings, funerals, daily services, holiday services, money matters, special holiday seating, accounting and, well, all that...You see?"

Jean-Pierre and Macha arrive in high spirits. They slide in among us. They already seem to know what was being discussed. Someone had not lost track and has filled them in. Everyone is staring at me, waiting for me to go on, like so many ethnologists on the scent of the unusual. In order not to disappoint them, I launch into it. I buy a round of drinks and then the show begins. You do not like this sort of theatre, Pascale, but I do. It does not bother me. It is the law of supply and demand. But you do not like the theatrics of selling oneself, I know, to an expectant audience.

You attempt a diversionary tactic. You turn toward them, and the long strands of light-coloured hair that brush along your cheeks steal my limelight. Your features betray a lovely, forced gaiety, an artfully prepared cocktail of charm: a full measure of playfulness, a pinch of candour, a dash of flirtation...And you begin to speak to those waiting in the wings while, under the table and unknown to them, your hand has begun to squeeze mine and has sent my inspiration plummeting:

"Hey, hold it just a minute! Tell me, would anyone be willing to lend me their notes from Michaux's course on Valéry?"

"Why did you leave the café in such a hurry last time?"

Your voice was filled with irritation. I felt compelled to justify myself.

"The last time...It was Friday...*Shabbat* falls early this time of year, in the autumn...I had to rush...to attend services."

"Are you as devout as all that?"

"Me? Oh no!...It was because of my parents..."

"If they're so devout, that's just fine...But to force you to run off to prayer services every Friday evening..."

"Devout...I don't think they're so devout, as you say. Devout is a Christian word. Let's just say that they're religious, that they practise their religion. That's more or less what it is. For us, you see, practising our religion is particularly important. It's my father's job, and consequently my mother's, too, and mine. We have to be there, to be present, to be seen."

"And faith, then?"

"Faith? Faith is another of your words, Pascale. One day you'll have to explain it to me."

The Latin prof's course is falling flat. We seem to bother the poor old man, and he certainly bothers us. Afterwards, we file out into the hall.

"I was upset with you for leaving like that. Not for me. For you. I have to tell you. Don't take just anyone home with you. As soon as your back was turned, Marc couldn't wait to tell us all about it, to describe in juicy and hilarious terms your extraordinarily 'primitive' and 'basic' way of life. He talked about you and your family as though he'd spent a month with a band of aborigines."

How harsh you can be. I feel like telling you: Pascale, you're being too hard on Marc. After all, it's hardly a serious matter.

"...Or else, if you don't see anything wrong with that, you're no better than he is."

Already you are turning your head away. Your anger is endangering our new-found relationship, our togetherness; your face has grown pale with annoyance and rage.

I would like to take you in my arms and hug and kiss your breath away. But I didn't. Why in the world didn't I?

"Listen, Daniel, no kidding, I want you to explain."

Explain? How can I, without giving the wrong impression without being too poetic — which would be false — or too sordid — which would not be accurate either — or too poetic and sordid at the same time — which would be a lie? I need a comparison, to compare it with something. But what? It comes to me all of a sudden.

"Have you seen *The Jazz Singer*?"

"What?"

"An old American film, the first talking film in the history of the cinema. One evening I went to see it at the Cinémathèque, because after all it's considered a classic. Just like everyone else in the theatre, I suppose, I was expecting a musical or a story about a black singer who finally sees his name in lights on Broadway. You know the billing: *All talking, All singing.* The first musical to hit the screen, something like that. Well, I was way off, it had nothing to do with a black singer — or a musical, for that matter. And it isn't even a comedy. It's the story of a young Brooklyn Jew living in a synagogue whose quarters have a window looking right down into the prayer room. It's a small apartment that he shares with his tired, old and apprehensive mother and with his father, who is extremely religious, who practises his religion in every way. He was hard. Frightening. I couldn't believe my eyes. In 1927, in Hollywood, a scriptwriter had already told my life story. Everything was there. The daily services and duties, the liturgical chants, the characters...And especially the décor: the same apartment, a little larger, perhaps, but so similar, right down to the furnishings, including the furniture, everything. I wondered whether he might have come here fifty years ago, to Paris, to our synagogue, to visit the secretary or the rabbi who preceded us...Because he must have been a Jew, the guy who wrote the story; he must have called upon what he had seen with his own eyes in order to tell it the way he did, a story played by Al Jolson and lived by me."

"But why the title, *The Jazz Singer*?"

"Because therein lies the hero's story, the drama. He has an ear for music and a beautiful voice. He's all set to succeed his father, to become a *hazzan*, a cantor in a synagogue, to assume the officiating functions, to be a good and pious Jew. But something happens along the way. He is attracted by the outside world, as we call it, by Broadway, which is only a few streetcar stops away. He can think of nothing but jazz, singing it and playing it. One day he leaves home, the small apartment above the House of God, in search of success, to lead a brilliant life, to make a name for himself. It's difficult at first, naturally; but little by little his fortune improves. In the meantime, he has fallen head over heels in love with a pretty little shiksa like you. His father finds out about it and his health begins to falter. For years the father will have nothing to do with him. Then, one evening, just prior to the opening of a show which was to make a star of him, he learns that his father is dying. He returns home, to his mother and to the apartment. Everything seems so strange to him, so sad, so difficult to understand...His reaction is very much like Marc's, without the irony, of course...In the end, he has to go down to the sanctuary to conduct services in place of his father, who is dying. What a strange setting for the first talking picture, a picture destined to be seen around the world. It could have been a western, a love story with Greta Garbo or even the career of a jazz singer, a real one! But it wasn't any of

those things, no more than I'm a bona fide modern literature student at the Nanterre campus."

And now you are sullen. You have not been taken in by
my bantering. Not at all. I have talked too much, or have
not expressed myself well. But it is the ignorance, the ignorance alone, which frightens you.

"Look, that old film is exaggerated. It's only an old film!
He wants to live his own life, he meets a...a shiksa, as you
say, and they kick him out, and then he returns just as his
father is dying. It's a bit...a bit..."

"...Melodramatic? That's what you mean, isn't it? Yes, the
moviegoers — and among them there were the most
ardent and best informed cinema enthusiasts, and those
who seem to know everything about everything — said
exactly that, that it was melodramatic, that the story wasn't
realistic at all, especially the setting. They found it absolutely impossible: a little world, separate, apart and in the heart
of New York City! In the twentieth century! For me,
though, it was the mirror image of my universe, a common,
everyday setting. It couldn't have been more real."

"And the things that happen to him are also realistic?"

"Yes, the things that happen to him, too. The things that
happen to him are all too probable, almost certain."

"Then...it would be very hard for you to change your life,
to lead your own existence, I suppose. With us, you see,
even the most devout people feel they owe their devotion
only to God. They don't have to answer to anyone else: not
to parents, not to the community...If what you say is true,
that means that if you loved a non-Jewish girl, you wouldn't
marry her..."

I am looking at the floor. I am telling myself that she insists on saying things she doesn't really understand. But she understands, all right, all too well. And I tell myself: Isabelle and I are dating; she wants to get engaged; she is sure to love me; that would surely be for the best; she is a true *yidishe meydele*...And yet there is nothing there; she has no idea of what or who I am; she does not even know who she is, even though her parents survived Dachau. She is intelligent and all, but this is how it is: Isabelle is tired of all that history. I do not love her now. I have never loved her. It is with you, Pascale, that I am falling in love, dangerously. Thank you, Pascale, for appearing not to expect anything of me, not yet, for allowing us to talk abstractly, at least a little while longer. And you will allow me a little duplicity too, I hope:

"No. That would be impossible. It wouldn't work. We would be too distant, too far apart. There would be things that a non-Jewish girl could never understand, never feel..."

You are staring at me intensely. I can no longer be sure whether you are sad or whether you are putting me on.

"And your parents would die if you did it, you believe that, don't you?"

"My parents. Oh, yes. There's no doubt. I've seen my mother and my sister in tears for days at a time, just because it happened to a distant cousin...It would kill them. They have told me so for such a long time and so often. If I have faith, as you put it, in anything, it's precisely that. By deserting them, I would kill them."

There is a long silence, and then you say, "Excuse me. I didn't mean to intrude. Forget what I said."

As you rushed off to class, you seemed a little too light-hearted, a little too playful all of a sudden.

I felt a strange happiness come over me at that moment, a feeling of liberation and audacity, as though all I had to do was pronounce aloud all my beliefs and they would disappear together into thin air. But you had already gone, and I was unable to share the event with you.

You are wise and prudent and patient. You kept me from speaking too soon. You gave me time.

You have given me an entire lifetime to think about it...

How strangely things turned out. One day you were no longer in a hurry. Our talks became a regular occurrence, endless, indispensable. You lent me some Ferré songs, daring and addictive — anything goes in a song, you said — then some by Bassiak, as exotically intoxicating as an Oriental liqueur.

I recall my surprise when you had me listen to those Ghetto songs. Anything goes in a song...Sarah Gorby's voice unsettled me. Why lead me back into all of that? By what right?

Spring was coming. We were threatened by the impending vacation.

Late one afternoon, we went up to my first student's quarters, to the room which, at your insistence, I had just rented for us. That was fine, except I had not succeeded in getting very far away from my childhood home. A pigeon could have made the trip from one rooftop to the other and back in less than a minute. How hot it was during those May days. How hot it was in my freshly painted garret, how bright and new and nude, as nude as we.

Marriage...Yes, we dared to pronounce the word. A very curious word indeed for the end of the sixties. No one around us even thought about getting married in those days.

But there was that day when you were almost run over by a truck. It was nothing serious, really, a little scrape on the forehead. Yet we started thinking about marriage, and the sooner the better. So we would be in the same family. So that if something happened to one of us, the other would know right away and would always be there to help and comfort.

Marriage. Nothing, no one could ever come between us. No one could send me off anywhere without you. We blessed the worldly compassion of the French Republic. We could get married at city hall, the mayor would be our rabbi and our priest.

I was still hopeful that there would not be a scene. And what if my parents did not die from it after all? And what if we ourselves suffered that fate because though we would be of the same flesh, there would be no one to recognize it?

Do you remember? Edith happened to be in Paris at that time...

And I thought that Edith...that in spite of everything...I thought...

Edith...No, Daniel, we are not going to talk about Edith. I know, I know, she was nine, she had crossed Europe as the last bombs were falling. You can still see it in her eyes, even today, how much she hates us for having been born after the bombing stopped, how much she hates us for being able to go to the university.

Seen too much. Too many anguished cries, too much fear. And here, in sunny Paris with us, amidst the carefree existences of so many others, she suddenly found herself lacking.

She had taken you by the hand when you were just a little baby; she told you time and time again about the man with the little moustache who had eaten all the Jewish children: "Except you and me, Damoel. So you see, we must never forget. We have to say *kaddish* for them all our lives. Damoel! Do you understand what I'm saying? Because, as a result, nothing beautiful, nothing bright, nothing peaceful can ever exist again. Never again on this planet."

How she must have hated the sun that day, hated the boulevard Saint-Germain, and the Café de Flore where we had taken her on an impulse. No, not impulsively; we thought it might put some of her demons to rest; we were counting on the absurdity of it, the futility of the tanned and flashy marionettes who go there to show themselves off, counting on that to calm her ghosts and to protect us from them. How she must have hated us for trying to look or be like them, even if only for a moment — the two of us, born after the bombing, going to the university...

And all the time that remained before us, the time that we claimed as our own, to which we had a right, the right to remain adolescents, whereas she...whereas she...

Seen too much. Too many anguished cries, too much fear. The three of us, she and you and I, in the cruel and futile Paris sun.

Daniel, you know full well...She did the best she could. She played along with us. She talked about this and that for as long as she could, as though she truly belonged to this peaceful and inane planet. Except there was the sun, and the tanned crowd on the terrace, and especially the two of us, and especially your hand on my shoulder, the two of us facing her, in tandem, acting out our happiness and our youth and demanding impunity, impunity from God, impunity from all the Dead.

Her eyes cried out: Damoel, Damoel, let her go, come back to us. And then you looked at me, and your hand crept from my shoulder to the back of my neck and began to caress my hair.

Her eyes cried out: Damoel, okay, keep her, it's already too late. Keep her if you must. But don't let her win you over. Damoel, I can't stand to see you with the peace in your eyes that I have never known. Keep her if you must, but lead her toward us. Come to us. My daughter Deborah will hold her veil beneath the nuptial canopy. And you can break the glass as they have broken our lives. And your children will be able evermore to say *kaddish* next to mine.

And our peaceful eyes told her no. No, never. We want to have our share here on earth. Our share. And nothing but ours. We don't want to be part of anyone else. We are lovers. We have to save our own skin.

She had her *kaddish*.

There she was, going to pieces in front of Le Drugstore, howling out the prayer for the dead at the top of her lungs before the frozen stares of so many connoisseurs of *chocolat liégeois*. There she was, seized in a hypnotic trance. I saw you suffer, Daniel, I saw you suffer, your eyes bulging with the ancient anguish that refuses to release you from its bondage.

The world, the real world, the one you thought you had touched, the simple world, benign, common, inoffensive, the everyday world that belongs to each of us, how very long it is taking you to learn about it.

$\mathbf{A}$fter that, we went to Sighet.

The living had decided that you no longer existed for them. So we decided to visit the dead.

Sighet. Do you remember, Daniel? The train station where we got off, the very one from which they had departed...

We were the only ones to get off there. Who would want to get off at Sighet? We had just spent eight hours on narrow, wooden benches, amazed to see the train slow to a stop when a peasant, loaded with poultry or sacks of wool, flagged it down in the middle of nowhere. And then a noisy giant appeared and invaded our compartment. We called them the Gauls, because their clothes looked so much like the ones worn by Vercingetorix's troops in our childhood history books.

Two hundred kilometres in eight hours. Our eyes had the time to take in the strange beauty of the soothing vastness, the immense plain stretching out and anticipating the mountains, Romania anticipating Russia...

Do you remember those loam farmhouses from which other "Gauls" would suddenly emerge half-naked? And do you remember that lovely girl with the long braids and flowing skirts, who, for next to nothing, sold us those wonderfully sour cherries wrapped in a newspaper?

One after the other, the Gauls got off the train. Soon we would be alone, you and I, the only passengers going as far as Sighet. Who goes to Sighet?

You remember, when the train finally stopped and we leaned out the door, we saw that sign: SIGHETUL MARMATEI.

So Sighet really existed.

You remember...We crossed the tracks hand in hand, and then walked out of the little empty station completely alone.

Who gets off at Sighet? Especially then, in 1967.

How should we go about seeing it? Sighet, a sleepy little town beneath a pure and brilliant sky.

It was hot that day. The sky was so pure and placid, with the mountains in the distance and the Tisza, the river where your father used to fish.

Everything is so serene in Sighet when the river is not swollen with bodies...

We had arrived. They all looked us over, tried to place us. The people of Sighet did not seem to be afraid of us. Probably because we were much too young to be returnees, not cven twenty yet, and therefore not old enough to hold anyone accountable. There were other factors: our matching blue jeans, our tee-shirts and English cigarettes, your hippie haircut. Both of us tanned and our hair bleached by the sun, at peace, we wandered aimlessly through Sighet — hand in hand. Two pure products of the West that people looked at with interest and, more often than not, smiled at. In 1967, absolutely everyone — including those tucked away in an isolated village in Transylvania — knew that Western youths had a strange passion for gallivanting around the world. They asked us where we were from. France, oh yes, Hugo, the Revolution. They asked us what we were doing. Sightseeing, we said.

Night was falling on Sighet. A warm breeze made it perfect for strolling. But we desperately needed to find a bed for the night. There was nothing available at the hotel; we should have booked reservations from Paris. We began to worry. English was no help, nor was French. Sighet is not exactly Romania. Everyone, or almost everyone, speaks Hungarian. So you decided to give it a try:

"*Kérem szépen, hol lehet egy szobát találni?*"

Silence. A heavy and crushing silence. So you insisted.

"A room. *Egy szobát.* Where we can spend the night. Tired. We are tired. We would like to sleep here."

Finally, we were directed to some kind of employee of some kind of town hall who motioned for us to sit down and asked you whether you had left during the 1956 crisis.

You said no, that you were born in France, that your parents were born in Austro-Hungary at the end of the reign of Franz Josef. They examined our passports for quite a while before making a phone call. One of them went with us, and we followed him through the streets and up a stairway to the third floor, where he introduced us to an old woman. She showed us to our room and said she was pleased the son of a true "Magyar" was staying with her...Then she left us under the protection of a phosphorescent Virgin, a replica of the one at Lourdes.

We stretched out next to each other in a large double bed beneath the hand-sculpted woodwork. We reached out and touched hands. We were a little frightened. We would not make love that night. Not there. The window opened onto the Sighet streets, and through it the warm and gentle Sighet night surrounded us. We thought about all of them. No. We did not think, we saw. Why must our eyes always be cameras?...We saw them in colour and in cinerama, all the ones you had never met but whose names you had retained, along with a few vague faces from the sparse photos. A few faces and Elie Wiesel, thanks to whose writings Sighet still existed, thanks to whom those who had left forever were known to us. Our Elie, who was still alive and who, thank God, was still so young...

Tell me, Daniel, what if that spring morning at the Sighet station had not taken place? When they were all taken away...who, what would you be? We think about them, we see them marching obediently along the street leading to the station...

And they, the departed, if they saw you tonight in this bed, holding hands with a *shiksa*...But it is true, I forgot. If they had not left, our lives would never have touched. Nothing would have been the same. There would not be a problem.

Tonight you and I are staying with the people who swept the town of Jews, then rushed to pillage and loot everything they could. We are staying with them, but it is not they we want to see. This trip is for the others, the ghosts. We have come all this way to ask them why they went along with it. Because that is what people have said to us, those of us who were born afterwards. Why did they let themselves be led like lambs to the slaughter?

Sighet. It was there that we understood. Sighet: a small town at the foot of the mountains, the vivid green of the plain, the purplish blue with which the squat houses are painted and repainted (that "*bleu de France*," the blue of our stained glass windows and, more recently, on packages of Gauloise cigarettes), the red of skirts and embroidery work.

Sighet: so far from everything. To understand, it has to be seen. It is an impervious place. It is a place where the rumblings of the world fall on deaf ears. There, people can believe only in the plain, the river and the mountains. Today, yesterday, always. Silence. Sighet and silence.

The next day we were up and about quite early: not a moment to waste, our transit visa was good for only two days on Romanian soil. We wandered around the tiny, sleepy-eyed streets. We did not dare ask for directions to the Jewish quarter or to the synagogues. Stretching out from Budapest, the iron curtain began to get to us: certain things are simply not mentioned, as we had become increasingly aware over the past few days.

We walked and walked. Without our accustomed mealtimes and routine pauses, the hours passed slowly and strangely in that disorienting strange place — disorienting, too, because we were searching with almost nothing to go on — only a few leins I had retained from Elie Wiesel's accounts, and what your father had told you, but your father couldn't tell you everything. Instinctively, we were drawn away from the centre of the town and toward other encounters and puzzles. We found ourselves in front of a pharmacy and decided to go in. We waited discreetly until all the customers had been waited on. Then, once we were the only ones left in the shop, the clerk turned toward us and attempted a few feeble words in French. You inquired:

"*Hol voltak a zsidó hazak?*"

He was tall and frail and tired. His eyes fell on us heavily. He seemed to be about to reply when an old peasant woman suddenly sauntered in. Then, taking you by the arm, he led you outside and said in a near whisper:

"There, there is where they lived."

We set out in that direction and, as we went along, examined every façade for a telltale sign: a double window in the form of the Commandment Tablets, any indication of a *yeshivah*. We walked along a street that looked different from the others. The houses were grouped tightly together on both sides of it, as though to form a barricade; the windows were barred and the entrances were protected by heavy double doors with grilled apertures for recognizing callers. Could the ghetto rich have lived here? Beyond that street, the quarter assumed a more middle-class character; the houses were still city dwellings of fortified construction, but one could sense the outlying presence of fields and the tranquillity of country life. Then, little by little, we moved away from those bastions designed to protect their inhabitants from pogroms. Soon, the houses were of that wonderful blue and resembled those we had seen dotting the farmlands.

It was there that we saw the poster. A small poster only slightly yellowed with age, a straw yellow, one might say, a rectangle surrounded by blue wall. And the printing had hardly faded.

It was Yiddish. Yiddish here, where no one read it any more, where no one spoke it — except you, who simply stumbled upon it one late afternoon. A poster that cried out bloody murder in echoes resounding back twenty-five years. And there we were, having travelled all that distance to see it, now staring at it, unable to move. Without stepping closer, you began to decipher it in a voice I could scarcely hear:

Brothers, they want us dead! Brothers! Do not be

deceived! For our deaths have already been decided. Let us take up arms and fight together.

A Zionist group? Or perhaps a few young people who no longer believed in divine protection? No doubt they had been our age...

That is what the poster said. A message put up there on that wall only a few days before the mass departure. Neither weather-beaten nor dog-eared. Only slightly yellowed. No one had thought to tear it down. But why tear it down? It no longer concerned anyone. They had all gone away. All of them.

All of them? Evening was coming upon us. A Friday evening. I wonder...*Shabbat*, could it be possible? While on vacation, one loses track of things — time and even the days of the week. It was *Shabbat* in Sighet, the evening hours. We had had nothing to eat or drink the entire day other than a beer. A little light-headed, we started back to the boarding house. We still had the following morning to discover whatever else might be there. The following day for the synagogues and the cemeteries. Yes, yes, we should wait until then. Besides, what was the point of searching? All Sighet is a cemetery. No. We would be better off to leave, to leave the dead behind and travel to Satu-Mare. Yes. We would look up that cousin whose address your father had given you. The following day would be for the living.

It was then that it happened. First there was a band of kids shouting out a litany with a recurrent phrase: *"Bolond Zsidó."* They were bounding around and gesturing in front of a half-opened door: *"Bolond Zsidó, Bolond Zsidó, Bolond Zsidó."* As our eyes moved upward, we saw it, the star. There was still a synagogue here after all. We went into the cool, moist darkness. Inside, there was one lone man coming and going and chanting all the while. We remained in the doorway and watched him go about things for a few long minutes, as the cries continued to echo around us: *"Bolond Zsidó, Bolond Zsidó..."*

Still there in the doorway, we found ourselves between the kids who were outside yapping in the reddening light of sunset and throwing a few stones but not daring to enter, and the man who continued to chant in the cool half-light of his temple.

To each his own litany.

We did not know whether to turn and leave or to step farther inside. Suddenly, he stopped and fell silent. We were face to face. He stared at us at length from out of the dim light, at our tanned faces and arms, at the sunglasses we now held in our hands. Out of instinct he addressed you, the one masquerading as a hippie; his voice whispered in Yiddish:

"Sholem aleykhem. A Yid?"

"Aleykhem sholem. Oui."

He motioned to us to come in. You showed him that you were bareheaded. He smiled sadly but welcomed us by lifting his hand in a gesture which signifies in every language: "My son, we are no longer concerned about such details."

He asked us where we were from. Paris, France. He continued the questions without much hope.

"Are there any Jews left in Paris? Are there any prayer gatherings, is there anything at all?"

You told him there were, and a good many.

"How many Jews?"

"A hundred thousand...Perhaps two hundred thousand."

He said, "*Nein,*" impossible. You tried to assure him. He asked whether you knew Yitzhak Lerner, and then he described him as he had been...before..Lerner

No, you did not know Yitzhak.

He shook his head. Yes. That's it. All of them. They are all dead. In Paris and everywhere else. People can say what they like. Nothing but stories. Everywhere it is the same, just like Sighet. And why should it be different? That's all there is to it. Here, for high holidays, there are still a few who come in from neighbouring areas. Just enough to make a *minyan,* as in Paris, no doubt. And everywhere else, too. He is the sole *Bolond Zsidó,* the last of the crazy Jews of Sighet.

He looked away; then his footsteps followed his gaze. "*Sholem aleykhem,*" he said as he resumed his prayers.

"*Aleykhem sholem.*"

But he stopped short and stepped back toward us. He looked at me intensely, then asked in a low voice:

"And she? Is she a Jew?"

You looked at me and nodded yes. She is also a Jew.

He smiled. Yes. Fine. No doubt. Besides, what would a *shiksa* be doing in Sighet? Yes...Yes, after all. There might well be two Jews left in Paris.

Summer would soon be upon us. We were planning to escape for a few months, to get as far away from all of them as possible, to lose ourselves in some out-of-the-way place where we could finally find ourselves.

When the noonday sun became too strong, we would close the fluted shutters amidst the sound of chirping crickets and, on a bed covered with thin bands of light, would make love. Months of making love, no schedules, no unnecessary precautions. Months of going about hand in hand, of kissing whenever and wherever we wanted to before benevolent or indifferent eyes.

We told our parents there would be a group of friends going with us. We talked about a trip to Italy, about historic monuments and culture. My parents seemed to go along with it. But yours, Daniel, despite your silence, yours suspected something from the very beginning and, at the last possible moment, they invoked their veto:

"You will go to Israel. It's been two full years since you set foot in that country. Besides, David has written and everything is arranged."

You came to our last rendezvous with your airline ticket in your pocket. Three months without seeing each other... How could we stand it?

My last trip to Israel...Do you remember, my love, how you wrote me letters addressed to just about everywhere in that country. You mailed them to virtually every general delivery department imaginable. And I wandered about from place to place on the trail of the kisses you sent air mail from anywhere between Brantôme and Bergerac.

That trip was so different from all the others. I went from here to there and back again, sometimes taking a room and other times sleeping on the beach. I had fallen out of grace with them. I was no longer the adopted son. Faded blue jeans and a light Indian tunic became my standard. I had lost weight and my hair had grown down the length of my deeply tanned face. Nadia made light of it; she recalled her own university years, her own escapades, then and now...All he could do was shout. So I had not wanted to carve out that proper and honourable place in the "Israeli way of life" that they had envisaged for me. I had deceived him, betrayed him. I had betrayed all of them. I had only come to play the tourist. And now I was playing at being a hippie.

His eyes shot blue darts. The son of a synagogue secretary, the grandson of a *shohet*, the great-grandson of a *shohet*, disguised as a bum, a Beatle, a hippie. He refuses the life of a free man in the sunshine of a new country.

His laughter echoed out into the heat of the night and across the other Tel Aviv balconies where, at that hour, everyone was taking the evening meal.

"Daniel Jonasz, a hippie, ha, ha!"

They were all there: the two sons, the daughters-in-law and the swarm of Sabra brats, models of conformity.

"Hip-pie, hip-pie," squalled the little towheads to the delight of the audience.

"A Jew. You will always be a Jew...But the point is" (there was a long pause while he endeavoured to make his eyes attain their maximum effect) "...the point is" (the sneering crease deepened on one side of his mouth), "do you know what you're doing in that get-up...and that hair? You see what I mean...A man, a real man, wears a simple white shirt and cuts his hair, if only so that people can distinguish him...from a woman."

I and the rest of the "Westerners" of that summer had to get used to being followed around by the jeers of two million provincial Israelis.

"Man or woman, man or woman?" chanted the model children, beside themselves with excitement.

"Quiet down, hush up, that's enough, you little brats! What do you know about anything? Leave him alone and finish your food! That's all that's expected of you."

Nadia had the courage to intervene. But already the patriarch had clenched his teeth and had begun to growl inaudibly. She shrank away, seemed to wither, to grow suddenly older and shapeless, too. She hid unmoving beneath the branches of the avocado tree, which after so many years was growing higher than the roof. My bag was packed and ready at my feet. I looked at all of them in anticipation of what was yet to come, the final proof that David wanted to have nothing more to do with me...

"Okay, okay, I'm almost finished," he began again. "Just one more thing: since it seems clear that you don't want to participate in the future of this country, since you're quite content with your silly university dreams, you should know at least this: the grandson of a *shohet* and the great-grandson of a *shohet* cannot go about disguised in that ridiculous manner. HE DOES NOT HAVE THAT RIGHT! GOT IT? Here, if you had wanted to, you could have gone about barcheaded and with your head still high. Like me, my children, my grandchildren...But since you prefer to remain there, the only future for you is to carry on the tradition, to help your father in his work, his obligations, his position in the community. There, that is the ONLY THING to do. Your escapades and unconventionality are illusions that will disappear of their own accord. You are to go back, cut that mop of hair, put on a clean shirt and return to services. Your father will find a position for you as a *shamash*...a *shohet*...an assistant secretary, whatever. That is the Jonasz tradition. That's all you can expect from life. No one else will hold out his arms to you."

So they have all made the same prediction. So Edith the Mad and David the Wise, both of them, have doomed me to the very fate that I have dreaded so much.

No one else will hold out his arms to you.

That is not true. I have you, my love, right here in the rear pocket of my jeans.

You sent me photos from the Basque coast, photos of you, lithe and so natural. Your eyes, which reflect a hint of the hardened sadness that comes with precocious maturity, plead with me to come back, offer me another way out. Now I have you, you whose face Nadia has seen. She sneaked a look at the glossy print and had just enough time to tell me this:

"That girl isn't just anyone. If you love each other, never forget, dear Daniel, to act according to your heart and your guts."

"But that's impossible, Nadia. She's a *shiksa*; my parents would die!"

"You think so! That's the same old song we play every time we think the children are getting away from us. It's just an old bogeyman. Don't worry, your parents won't die; it won't be fatal. Just like everyone else, they will die from disease or old age."

She told me that in a rapid voice as I started down the stairs to get away. She told me so I would know that though she was tired and powerless and a little faint-hearted, she had remained silent during a scene of which she did not approve.

Afterwards, I went down to the beach where I looked at your photos until nightfall stole them from view. Then I fell asleep on the warm sand.

I am coming back, my love. There is nothing else to do here. But I am afraid. I am afraid they may be right. You know they all said the same thing...And what if it is true...? What if I really have no other choice?

Suddenly I am afraid to see you again. Afraid that your arms will never be enough to replace all those extra families I have persisted in collecting over the years.

Do not be too optimistic. Do not overestimate your strength. Perhaps you and Nadia are wrong; perhaps heart and guts are not enough to be a good Jew. Perhaps a good Jew needs other things: a mind, to study, to analyze, to reason, to react in time; perhaps a good Jew also needs an immense family, tyrannical yet forever welcoming; perhaps a good Jew even needs the entire community in order to feel secure...Yes, that community which has been responsible for so much of my suffering but which also has always been ready, for thousands of years, to welcome back the prodigal son.

Should I really take the next plane back? Will you have the strength to replace all that? And will your arms be enough?